To Ji'

MW01128783

THE SELKIE PRINCE'S
FATED MATE

THE ROYAL ALPHAS, BOOK 1

J.J. MASTERS

Happy Reading!

Jeanne St James

xoxo

JJ Masters

J.J. MASTERS

––––––––––

Thank you to my beta readers:
Author Whitley Cox, Nessa Kreyling, Sharon Abrams,
and Arlyna Fischer

JOIN J.J.

To keep up with J.J. and her upcoming books, please join her readers' group on FB here:

https://www.facebook.com/groups/JJMastersAuthor/

Join her newsletter here:

https://bit.ly/2E2zcaB

Or keep an eye on her website:

http://www.jjmasterauthor.com

CHAPTER ONE

THE BLOOD RUSHED to Kai's cock as he took a long, deep inhale.

This Presentation Ceremony was unnecessary. As were all the last dozen or so. There was no reason to have six omegas from all over the country—and even some from Europe—presenting themselves to him each time.

All to find his fated mate.

No matter what, it was clear. The *pater* of his future pups was now present in the Great Hall. He was one of the six males naked on their hands and knees, their foreheads pressed to the cold stone floor, their asses high in the air.

The second Kai had entered the hall, his omega's slick glands had started to express themselves. It was hard to deny the scent his future mate gave off.

His hatred for these presentation ceremonies burned within him like the heat of a thousand suns. How insulting to be an omega from a good family and be forced to be on display in front of many, many other males in the hall and postulating in front of the reigning King of the North.

His sire, King Solomon.

The ruling Selkie male loved this pomp and circumstance. Kai despised it.

His father sat on his throne at the head of the hall, wearing not only his damn crown, but holding his scepter.

His freaking scepter.

But like it'd been told to Kai countless times before, it was all for the good of the race.

Sure.

Being the oldest son of five, he was next in line for the throne.

Not that he wanted it, because he didn't.

Not that he had a choice. He certainly didn't.

Just like he wouldn't have a choice in choosing his future mate. That would be chosen for him due to the fates. An omega he'd have to spend the rest of his life with, who would sit by his side if and when Kai ever reigned the kingdom, and who would bear his pups.

No, Kai's body would decide that.

So, he had no choice. None. And neither did his omega.

Kai hoped he at least found his bonded mate easy on the eyes, and somewhat intelligent. Otherwise, he wasn't sure if he'd be able to tolerate being tied to a male Kai couldn't bear to look at, breed with, or even have a decent conversation with.

That would seem like eternal torture.

Kai's nostrils flared as the sweet, luring scent of his bonded mate became stronger. His cock was now more painful than ever.

He didn't think he'd ever gotten this hard with any of his beta or human lovers.

"Son, come forward," his father's deep voice encouraged. Hell, *demanded.*

Kai frowned at all the formality. The Royal Guards lined both sides of the hall, leaving him a clear path to the throne, the "presentation," and his four brothers. Two stood on one side of their father, two on the other.

They looked as uncomfortable as Kai felt and Zale was giving him an intense stare that read, "Hurry up and choose, so we all can get the bloody hell out of here."

Kai understood that sentiment well.

With a sigh, Kai moved forward, his eyes traveling over the bare asses being presented for everyone to see.

Thanks be to Poseidon, he was grateful that he was not an omega.

His nose wrinkled and twitched as he strolled down the line behind them. But his attention kept being drawn to the omega on the end.

That was him. His mate. His future.

Kai's life as he knew it was now over. The Seekers had finally found his mate. He purposely rounded the group and then, crossing his arms behind his back, he marched down the line in the front.

Because to do so was expected. And, of course, by doing what was expected would keep his father's ire at him to a minimum. Staying off the king's radar was something he and his brothers have worked hard at since they were young pups.

Kai took shallow breaths through his mouth, so his omega's scent wouldn't overwhelm him. He certainly never smelled anything like it.

Admittedly, it was heady. It made his heart race and his cock twitch. And the strong instinct to mount and rut his omega right then and there made his mind spin.

He could just imagine what his father would say if Kai reduced himself to acting like nothing more than a horny dog humping a human's leg.

Kai was a bit worried that it may actually happen if they didn't hurry up and get this "ceremony" over with.

No one had explained to him just how strong his instincts to rut would become once he found his fated mate. It was quite disturbing since it made his control teeter on a dangerous edge. He gritted his teeth and twisted his fingers together behind his back to make sure he remained upright on his two feet as well as fully clothed.

Even though he knew he didn't have to get close to figure out which male was his mate, he approached the one on the end, the light-haired one with the eyes tipped down to the floor. Those sea green eyes had flicked up in defiance just long enough for Kai to see that fascinating color. And it was the color that drew him in.

But it wasn't only the unique shade of his eyes. Kai could scent his future mate, the one whose body went still and solid as Kai gave in and bent over, grabbing the omega's elbow and drawing him to his feet.

His omega stood, eyes still tipped—in what Kai assumed was feigned submission—to the floor. He stepped closer to touch the tip of his nose to the soft skin behind the omega's ear at his scent gland and inhaled deeply.

The omega's alluring and somewhat sweet, but strangely familiar scent, filled his nostrils and lungs as his skin began to tingle. His body became warmer and his cock began to engorge.

His reaction surprised him because the male who stood before him wasn't even in oestrus yet. With the way Kai's body was reacting now, he couldn't imagine how crazy out of his mind he'd become once the male went into heat.

Even so, with that one breath, Kai reflected once more that his life would never be the same again. He was going to be tied to this stranger for the rest of his days on Earth and in the Great Sea. He would now only mate with this single being and this male would be tasked to produce his heirs.

Once more, he hoped he liked this omega and could bear to live with him, otherwise he was screwed. If not, he'd have to do his duty with this fated mate and find his pleasure, his sexual release, elsewhere. A beta. A human. Whoever.

"Son..." his father called from behind him.

Ignoring the annoyance in his father's voice, he stared down into those sea green eyes, now bravely meeting his, and asked, "What is your name?"

The male before him shuddered but stared with unexpected confidence at Kai. "Loukas. But I go by Luca."

Kai watched the omega's full, soft lips move as he spoke. He could almost imagine the warmth of his breath brushing along Kai's skin as they rutted.

"Luca," Kai murmured softly, not only mesmerized by the male's mouth, but by those eyes of his which peeked from between thick, golden lashes. "Bringer of light."

Luca tilted his head slightly. "If you say so, Your Royal Highness."

Kai frowned. "Don't call me that again," he snapped sharply.

Luca tipped his head down, his captivating eyes following at a slower pace. "I beg your pardon, sir." The male was obstinate, unfearful and his demeanor didn't match his apology.

Kai liked it.

"Son!" his father yelled from his position at the head of the hall, thumping the bottom of his scepter onto the stone platform several times to get Kai's attention. "*Prince Kai.*"

The king only called him that when he was irritated. Which seemed to be often.

Kai sighed and muttered, "Shit."

He didn't miss Luca flattening his lips before Kai turned to face his father. Not that he wanted to since his erection was now raging and there'd be no possible way to hide it.

"Yes, sire?" he asked with his own feigned obedience.

Suddenly, his father's assistant, Douglass, was fluttering around him like a hummingbird on crack.

"Your Highness... Please. There are certain steps that must be taken..."

Kai swatted his hand at Douglass, wishing the male *was* as small as a hummingbird so he could knock him to the ground and stomp him with his boot. The Northern Colony would be a better place without that little pest.

"I know, Dougie," Kai said wryly. "You've gone over them with me a million times. I just don't feel like following your steps."

"They're not *my* steps, Your Highness. They're tradition—"

Kai cocked a brow at Douglass. "And since when have I ever followed tradition?"

"If you're going to take a mate—"

"Do I *have* to take a mate?" Kai glanced over his shoulder back at Luca. "Sorry, nothing personal." Then he let his gaze roam down the male's body. Only for a second, though. He'd inspect him closer later. When he had a lot more time. And he could do something to relieve the ache in his balls.

Douglass grabbed his elbow, making Kai freeze and look down his nose at the little pest. The assistant released him quickly, taking a step back, color flooding his pale cheeks.

"You forget yourself, Dougie," Kai growled.

"I... I'm sorry, Your Highness."

Kai raised his gaze from the smaller male to the head of the Great Hall. His father sat holding that damn scepter tightly with white-knuckled fingers, his face pinched and red, his eyes narrowed. Kai's gaze bounced over to his brothers from left to right...

Zale, who had his head dropped and his body shaking with laughter. He *would* find this all amusing. Marlin, who stood with his arms behind his back, staring at the ceiling, probably with impatience. Caol, who was too busy eyeballing a handsome beta guard. One of a few that lined both sides of the hall.

And then there was Adrian, standing there in typical Rian style, pretending to act bored but Kai knew his brother from another mother... err, *pater*... was annoyed as much as their father.

Rian tended to take this kind of shit seriously, as well. Being the second oldest, he probably prayed to Poseidon every night for something to happen to Kai to make him the next reigning King of the North instead of his older brother.

Funny. Kai sort of wished that, too.

But he hoped it wasn't his demise that made it so. He kind of liked breathing and living life.

"Father, I've found my mate," Kai announced in a bored tone. "So, can we just dispose of all this unneeded," he waved his hand around the air, "sh— garbage?"

"Yes, Father, it's almost time for dinner and I'm starved," Marlin drawled.

"You've found your mate, just like that?" the king boomed. "You aren't supposed to go up to them and simply start sniffing, Kai."

"But I don't have to sniff them. I can clearly recognize my mate's scent. Isn't that the way it's supposed to work? Anyway, he's here. And if you haven't noticed, he's the one standing there naked. Can we at least get him some clothes and send the rest of them on their way?"

King Solomon sighed with loud exaggeration. "Kai, you will be the death of me yet."

"No, I'm pretty sure that will be Caol."

His youngest brother shot Kai a smirk.

"Douglass," the king boomed out. "You may send the others away. Make sure to send their families the obligatory gift along with our deepest gratitude."

Like little Dougie needed his father to tell him what to do. The assistant took his job seriously and did his best to anticipate any of his father's needs.

Which were many.

Douglass did a deep bow. "Yes, Your Highness."

When he rose, Kai pointed to the beta's face. "Dougie, I think there's a little brown spot at the end of your nose," he said just loud enough for Douglass and his brothers to hear.

Douglass wiped at it quickly, frowning when he found nothing.

A sharp snort came from Zale. And Caol looked about ready to explode.

King Solomon slammed the end of his scepter down on the stone floor once more. "Enough!"

"Father, you know Kai doesn't take anything seriously," Rian said dryly.

The king made a noise of impatience. "I'm well aware of that." He pinned his narrowed gaze on Kai. "This is not a joke, *Prince Kai*. This is not only important to our royal bloodlines, our kingdom, and our colony, but our Selkie race as a whole."

Oh, no pressure. No, none at all.

Kai tilted his head toward the king. "Thank you for reminding me of that, Father. If you'd like, my new-found mate and I can go get to know each other a little better right now and get an immediate start on saving our kind. You know, for the good of our race."

Marlin now stared at his feet, shaking his dark head and hiding his grin.

"You know what comes next," King Solomon said through gritted teeth.

Yes, Dougie had said that if the Seekers were ever successful on finding his mate, after the naked ass presentation would come a meal.

Like a repast after a funeral.

"We will all head directly to the dining hall and break bread with the newest member of our royal family," his father finished and then clapped his hands loudly. "Douglass! Come bring the boy his clothes!"

Oh joy. Kai got to sit next to his mate and inhale his intoxicating scent as they sat around a table a mile long and tried to make polite small talk and eat.

He doubted he'd be able to concentrate on food.

He'd rather take his omega back to his wing in the castle, so he could get to know Luca better.

He wasn't kidding his father about being willing to get started on saving their kind. Or at least going through the motions. Since his mate wasn't currently in heat, there'd be no possible way for Luca to get pregnant. But it would be fun to try, anyway.

He had no idea how he was going to sit through a formal dinner consisting of five courses with his current predicament. Which was his painful erection.

As he raised his eyes to the throne, he saw his father smiling at him. The king knew exactly what reaction Kai was suffering by him being so close to his omega and not being able to mark him fully as his yet.

King Solomon was enjoying this. And that knowing smirk he wore clearly said, "Paybacks are a bitch."

CHAPTER TWO

LUCA WANDERED around the large suite feeling a little over-whelmed. He had been brought here by a beta servant right after finishing dinner. Not that he had eaten much since his stomach had been tied in knots.

How could it not be? He had sat for two long hours next to his new alpha. Imagine that! *His* fated mate turned out to be an actual prince and next in line for the throne as the King of the North.

That meant whatever heirs he produced with this prince could eventually succeed the throne. Whatever pups he bore would be princes in their own right.

But that wasn't what made him slick with excitement. No, that wasn't it at all. It was the alpha himself.

Being raised in a family of good breeding, Luca always knew that it could be possible he'd end up being the fated mate for an alpha of nobility. Who and where he never knew. As soon as he had become "of age," the Selkie Seekers had summoned him time and time again to present him to royalty of all levels. From a king all the way to the lowest level of Selkie nobility, a baronet.

He couldn't say he enjoyed any of the presentations. They were somewhat humiliating. However, over the last ten years, he'd gotten used to them. Well, as much as he could get used to being nude in a head down, ass up position in front of a crowd. Sometimes for up to an hour at a time.

Each time he was summoned he had hoped he wouldn't get stuck with some unbearable, abusive or very unattractive alpha. Because if he did, he knew he had to do his duty no matter what and rut with whomever it was. As an omega, he didn't have a choice to turn away the mate fates handed him.

It was his obligation and, more importantly, it was the law. If he refused, he and his family would be banished from any and all Selkie communities. They would become outcasts.

However, as soon as Prince Kai had entered the Great Hall of the North, he knew that the male was· his alpha. Luca's slick glands had started to leak just slightly, and his hole had loosened in preparation for mating. At that point, it took all that Luca had to remain in place, to stay in his submissive position as the alpha strode around them, inspecting the offering of omegas.

Of course, Luca had snuck in some peeks here and there and was pleased to find that his alpha was in his prime. Tall, broad-chested, dark-haired, and... simply handsome. When the regal prince had brought Luca to his feet, he'd lost his breath as he stared into those Caribbean blue eyes. The ones that bore straight into his soul.

Luca had been overcome with relief that his alpha was not only easy on the eyes but not much older than him. And from what he could tell over dinner, even though conversation was a bit difficult with the table being so long and the royal family being so spread out, his alpha seemed to be intelligent.

He also appeared to have a good relationship with his younger brothers. From what Luca learned before coming to the Northern Colony was that all of King Solomon's sons had different *paters*. And that the king currently had no omega at all. They had all died while delivering pups, whether while whelping the current princes or siblings that also perished along with the *pater*.

From how the stories went, Prince Kai's *pater* had died while whelping him and the firstborn prince was raised by a female human nanny who wet-nursed him. One from the local sea town not far from the colony.

While human nannies weren't unheard of, especially for nobility, it wasn't the norm. Most times other betas were used. However, using a lactating female human as a wet-nurse was something simply not done, at least out in the open. Normally, if an omega mate died while whelping, or shortly after, another lactating omega stepped in to help feed the infant pup.

Apparently, King Solomon liked to do things differently. And although he had lost five omega mates, and none were knocking down his door to be the sixth, he still managed to produce five impressive heirs.

Luca spun on his heels as the oldest entered the large suite.

"Did Vin give you a tour of my wing?"

His alpha's deep, rich voice sent a shiver sliding down Luca's spine.

Vin must be the beta who introduced himself as Kelvin before bringing Luca back here after dinner.

Luca stiffened his spine, so he wouldn't melt into a puddle at the prince's feet and beg for the alpha to take him. "Yes, he was quite kind and helpful."

Luca inhaled deeply which caused a flutter in his belly as Prince Kai nodded and moved closer. A look crossed the prince's face, then he quickly stepped away, giving them both some needed space. "We'll have plenty of room. My quarters are large, so we won't have to live on top of one another."

Luca wouldn't mind his alpha being on top of him right now.

He squeezed his butt cheeks together as he felt another trickle of slick escape.

Luca cleared his throat and asked, "Does each prince have their own wing like you?" in an attempt to keep his mind off the large bed in the room right off the living area they stood in presently. He only got a quick peek at it when Kelvin gave him the nickel tour. When he had time, he'd explore the rest of the prince's wing, or quarters, more thoroughly on his own.

"Yes. They're large enough to accommodate not only our mate but our future heirs."

"I see you even have your own kitchen, so you don't have to dine in the dining hall."

"The dining hall is only used for formal meals. We each have our own beta servant, but more often than not, my brothers and I dine together either here or in one of their wings."

"And does the king join you?"

"Normally not," his alpha answered in a flat, lifeless tone.

Luca simply nodded, not sure how to respond to that. Luca loved both his father and his *pater,* and he couldn't imagine not wanting to spend time with them both. In fact, this would be the first time living apart from them.

He hoped Prince Kai wouldn't mind them visiting from time to time or would kindly allow Luca to visit them occasionally even though they didn't live close by.

"Luca," Prince Kai said softly, making Luca's head swing in his direction. Their gaze met, and tingles ran down his spine once more at the heated look his alpha gave him.

"Yes, Prince Kai?" Luca asked just as softly, his breathing becoming shallow and a warmth radiating from his belly to his crotch. Another trickle of slick slipped from him.

But the prince's next question made him freeze.

"Have you been presented before?"

KAI STUDIED the future *pater* of his pups and held his breath as he waited for an answer.

"Yes."

The air rushed out of him and an unexpected prickle of jealousy skittered down his spine. Not only was it unexpected, it was an unfamiliar feeling. He'd never had a reason to be possessive of his beta or human lovers. They were just that. Lovers. Nothing more. Nothing less.

But not all nobility was in the market for a fated mate. Sometimes they were just looking for an omega mate or simply a breeder. Especially if their fated mate couldn't be found or had died either in whelp or perished for another reason. Or their fated mate was infertile. And that was when the mate could be cast aside for another. Nobility were required to produce heirs one way or another. They had to take another mate if their fated one couldn't be located or couldn't produce an heir.

Luca could have very well been claimed by another prior to being presented to Kai. And though that thought shouldn't bother him because he hated forced traditions, it strangely did. Kai might never had met the omega the fates had destined for him if that had happened.

It was up to the Seekers to decide when the search for a royal's fated mate would be over. And it wasn't until then could the royal choose another.

"To who?"

"To Laird Daividh."

Fascinating. "Hmm. Scotland."

Luca shifted uncomfortably, his gaze landing on a spot somewhere behind Kai.

"And who else?" Kai prodded, curious at his reaction.

"And King... Egbert."

Kai's head jerked back in surprise. "King Egbert? The Brit?"

Luca closed his eyes. "Yes."

Kai's eyebrows rose. "Interesting. Aren't you a little old for King Egbert? I heard he likes them... *young.*" So young his choice of omega mates would be considered illegal by human law standards.

"He does."

"And he already found his fated mate from what I understood."

"He did."

Kai eyed Luca. "So why is he still searching? It's not like there's more than one fated mate out there for us alphas." Or was there? He'd always been told there was only one. And when you found your omega, *the* omega, that was it.

Or had that been a lie?

"His fated mate died in whelp."

Kai was surprised he hadn't heard that news. "Did the pup survive?"

"He did."

"But Egbert wants more heirs."

"He does," Luca confirmed. "Just like King Solomon..." he trailed off.

"Yes, just like my father, who I consider the Black Widow of our race. Do you know not one of my brothers has the same *pater*? My *pater* was the king's true fated mate and when my *pater*..." Kai let his words fade away. He only met Luca a few hours ago. There was no reason to dump a bunch of bitterness on the poor male. This entire process had to be overwhelming to him as it was.

Luca bowed his head slightly. "Yes, Your Highness. I'm aware."

Kai sucked in a breath. As much as he disliked the formality, he hated it even more when it was used in his own personal quarters. Even Vin was permitted to call him by his first name and not his title when tending to him in private. "Please don't call me that."

Luca startled him when he stepped up to Kai, almost toe to toe, and met his gaze directly. A very confident move. "You are my alpha. Please tell me what you would like me to call you, then."

Luca being this close was dangerous. His sweet scent swirled around him. "Kai."

"Just Kai?" Luca asked, his brows raised.

Kai stared down into those sea green eyes and felt himself drowning. "Yes," he whispered. "Just Kai."

"Will that be acceptable outside of our quarters?" Luca asked in a similar whisper.

Our quarters.

It hit Kai that he now had a permanent roommate.

"Yes. And if anyone has a problem with it, including the king, you let me know. Now, as for inside our wing..." Kai dropped his head until his lips were barely above Luca's. His nostrils flared as he inhaled that sweet, fragrant scent and he stared at the male's soft, full lips. "You may call me whatever you'd like. Except for Your Highness."

"Even 'my bull?'" Luca murmured in a slightly breathy but teasing tone.

Hmm. Did he remind Luca of a bull seal? Confident and quite dominant, a bull seal claimed what was his and would fight to the death to keep it. Now that his omega stood before him, he could see himself easily fitting that description. It wasn't unheard of that a Selkie alpha would be called a bull, especially during his omega's heat cycle. An omega's oestrus could turn an alpha just as savage as a wild bull seal.

So, would he mind Luca calling him a bull?

Kai's cock kicked in his pants and his lips curled up at the ends. "Yes, even that. If you feel inclined to yell out 'Fuck me harder, my bull' when we're rutting, I certainly won't stop you."

Luca sucked in a breath. "Will I get the opportunity to yell that soon?"

"If you wish it."

Luca nodded, holding Kai's gaze. "I do," he returned softly, his warm breath sweeping over Kai's lips.

Kai dropped his mouth to Luca's and his hands dug into the omega's dark blond hair, tilting his head back and slipping his tongue between those soft, full lips. The tips of their tongues touched, then tangled.

A groan bubbled up from the back of Luca's throat as Kai took complete control of Luca's mouth, exploring every inch. With a slight twist of his head, he took the kiss deeper. He was pleased Luca didn't resist him. Though, maybe Luca should.

Even though Kai knew they weren't permitted to rut before their official bonding ceremony, that was all he wanted. His throbbing cock pressed against Luca's lower belly since the omega was a good six inches shorter.

Kai broke the kiss, shoving his nose against the scent gland behind Luca's ear and inhaling deeply, his breathing ragged and quick. Holding his mate tightly against his body, he was pleased he could feel Luca's erection against his hip. The attraction was clearly mutual.

Kai slid a hand down Luca's back and his long fingers dipped into the back of the omega's waistband. He simply wanted to slip a finger down there to see just how slick, how aroused his mate was. But if he did that, if he felt how wet Luca was, he may not be able to stop himself from dragging the male into the bedroom and having his way with him. Instead, he jerked away and stepped back, curling his fingers into fists. Closing his eyes, he took a few harsh breaths in an attempt to control his urges.

"We can't," Kai said, his words strangled. He rushed to a

window at the other end of the living area, pressed his hands against the glass and stared out. "Bloody hell," Kai barked, the glass pane nearest his face fogging up from his outburst.

"I'm sorry, Prince Kai... Sorry, *just Kai*. Did I do something wrong?"

Kai shook his head but remained facing the window. "No. Nothing on purpose. You are tempting me... Your scent."

"I'm sorry... I..."

"It's not your fault. *None* of this is your fault. It's these bloody *traditions*," he spat out.

"You mean not consummating our bond until after the official ceremony?"

"Yes," Kai growled. "I cannot mark you as mine until afterward."

Kai's heart raced at his own words. *I cannot mark you as mine.*

Well, he *could*. He was a prince after all. And the only male he really had to answer to was the king, his own father. And *maybe* the Royal Council. But once Luca was marked as Kai's, their scents would be mingled and anyone at the bonding ceremony would be able to tell that Luca and Kai had mated before they were allowed.

And by doing such, Luca may be looked down upon by not only his brothers but the king himself as being loose and easy. Not a good way to begin his integration into the Royal Family. Being known as a Selkie slut was certainly not an endearing quality and Kai would rather not burden Luca with that all because Kai couldn't control his own selfish urges.

But oh, it was tempting. Very tempting.

"Can I ask when this ceremony is scheduled?"

Kai glanced over his shoulder, a lock of hair falling over his forehead, to see that Luca had taken a few steps closer. The omega's thoughts must be barreling like a freight train in the same direction as Kai's. "Are you as anxious as I am?"

"Yes, Your Highness... Prince Kai..." Luca winced at his blunder. "*Kai.*"

Kai stared at his omega mate for a moment while willing his blood to flow in the direction of his brain instead of his cock. "I don't know why Vin brought you back to my quarters."

"Was he not supposed to?"

Kai blew out a breath, then he cursed loudly, "For the love of Poseidon!" making Luca jump.

Luca's eyes widened as Kai rushed him before he could stop himself and hauled his omega against him. He stared down into those sea green eyes which were now mostly black because his pupils were so large. Kai's erection was hot and heavy as a moan slipped from Luca's lips.

But it was Luca this time who found the strength to remind Kai that they needed to wait by whispering, "How soon is the ceremony?" Which also reminded Kai that he never answered the question the first time. His brain was truly addled.

Kai cupped Luca's cheeks for a moment then forced himself to move away once again, berating himself for being so weak.

He never hated being a prince more than at that moment. If they had been Selkies of the common kind, just any alpha and omega, they would have had the bonding ceremony immediately and mated already. No fuss, no muss.

He glanced at his watch and groaned silently. After Vin had escorted Luca back to Kai's quarters, Douglass had rushed into the dining hall announcing that everything was set for the bonding ceremony which would begin promptly at eight.

Eight.

It was only seven-thirty and Kai didn't know how he would be able to resist his leaking omega for another thirty minutes. Maybe he should leave and go walk around the compound.

Inhale some fresh sea air. Take a quick dip in the frigid November surf.

But he couldn't leave. He couldn't. Something pulled at him to remain by his omega's side, to protect him, to make sure Luca was not left alone near any other alphas, including his brothers, until he was fully marked and claimed.

"Why can't I..." Kai frowned. "Quit you?"

Luca made a noise that sounded like a laugh and cocked a brow in Kai's direction. "Why can't you *quit* me?"

His omega laughed at him, which made Kai's frown deepen. He hadn't meant for that question to slip out, but his mind had turned to mush.

"Is that a *Brokeback Mountain* reference?"

Kai sighed and rolled his eyes toward the ceiling. "Maybe."

Luca grinned. "Did that movie make you cry, too?"

"Mmm," Kai murmured.

Luca's laughter sounded like music to Kai's ears. Curse the sea gods, he was truly becoming infatuated with the male.

"Wow. Who would have thought that my alpha bull would be such a softie?"

Kai pinned his gaze on Luca. "That doesn't leave this room," he growled.

"And if it does? Then what?"

"Then your 'bull' will see red and your ass will match it." Bloody hell, he hadn't meant for *that* to slip out either.

"Hmm. Tempting." Luca grinned again. "So, it's nice to hear even royalty watches movies like us common folk. Do you have a Redbox in some corner of this kingdom?"

"No. It's called Netflix."

"*Ah.* Even better. Like to Netflix and chill, my bull?"

My bull. The male before him was certainly insolent. Kai raised his brows. "Do you?"

Luca lifted one shoulder lazily as he answered, "Never had a mate before."

Of course not. But that didn't mean he was a virgin. "But you've had lovers." Kai didn't make that a question on purpose. But he definitely wanted an answer.

"Have you?"

Touché.

Kai tilted his head and studied his fated mate. "Mmm. Yes."

"Other omegas?"

Kai did not need to answer any of Luca's questions. He was the alpha here. He was a prince. But he did have to live with him for the rest of his life. *Technically.* So it wouldn't hurt to "bond" with him more than sexually, especially before the ceremony. "No, never other omegas. I couldn't risk sending an omega into heat."

"Fearful of whelping a bastard pup? Or two?"

"No. Fearful of being stuck with someone who wasn't *the one.*"

Luca's eyebrows rose in question. "The one?"

Yes, the one who smells as sweet and alluring as you. "My mate."

"Me," Luca stated.

"Yes, you," Kai confirmed.

"I know it's the 'way' of our race, to have fated mates to ensure the continuation of our kind. But do you find it odd to be stuck with someone you don't know and must breed with for the rest of your life?"

"Stuck with?" Kai hesitated, then shrugged in answer. He continued, "But *must* breed with? No. I'm only obligated to breed with you until you're carrying my pup. I only need to satisfy my *obligation.*"

"Just one," Luca murmured.

"Yes. One." An alpha pup that lives, Kai added silently. No

one knew better than Kai how dangerous whelping could be for an omega. He and his brothers had all lost their *paters* that way. All of them. And a few sibling pups along with them.

While omegas had evolved to bear pups, they still weren't the ideal vessel for carrying and whelping them. They had developed over time out of the necessity of continuing their race, but evolution was not perfect. And it might be hundreds of years before the omega birthing process became less dangerous for the *pater*.

"And after?"

"After that? I have other options."

Luca's jaw got tight. "Other options," he repeated slowly with a slight frown, as if that concept left a bitter taste in his mouth.

There was no reason to lie to this omega. He needed to know what his future might consist of. "We have a stable of sorts consisting of willing betas at our disposal. Volunteers who get to live here in the castle and enjoy a pampered life in exchange for their *services,* if you will. However, there are also... humans... in town."

"Humans?" Luca spit out with distaste.

"Yes. Humans. Don't knock them if you haven't tried them."

"Will I have the same options as you once I whelp your *obligated* pup?"

Kai studied the omega in front of him. "Do you think you'd get the same freedoms as me?"

"Why not? Because you're a prince?"

"No, because I'm an alpha. Not just any alpha, but *your* alpha. Need I remind you of that?"

Color rushed into Luca's face. It was cute. The omega was extremely easy on the eyes, thank the great sea gods. His body was lean, and though Kai had tried hard not to stare at him when Luca was naked in the Great Hall "presenting" himself head down, ass up, he had snuck in a few glances. He was looking forward to when he could study his fated mate's naked body at his leisure. In private. Up close and personal.

"We've not had a chance to get to know each other yet, and I wanted to give us that chance. But if you need a reminder, Omega, there are things I can do to you that no one else will be able to tell what's been done. Is that what you'd like?" Like turning his sweet omega's ass a bright shade of red.

Luca bowed his head, his eyes tipping down but not completely to the floor.

Yes, his handsome omega was obstinate. *Hmm.*

Even so, Kai was relieved the male wasn't spineless. Because if he had been, Kai would only do his duty until his fated mate produced an heir then he'd be tossed aside. Kai could not tolerate weakness in his race. Omega or not. Beta or not.

Though creatures of the sea, Selkies in general were not a weak species. And he'd be disappointed if his son was born to a *pater* that was. That trait could be passed on.

For his kind to continue to survive, they needed the best and strongest to breed. If not, his race would perish. Only to become a distant memory. There were fewer Selkie colonies now than there were hundreds of years ago. So it wasn't only important for the royalty among the kingdoms to breed, but everyone who was capable had a duty to produce healthy, happy pups.

It was their law.

That thought brought his attention back to the omega in front of him.

"You're leaking," Kai murmured then winced. *Oh bloody hell!* He hadn't meant for *that* to come out, either. He was losing his damn mind.

Luca's sea green eyes widened, then darkened and became hooded. "You know that, how?"

Kai's nostrils flared. "By your scent."

Luca sniffed the air. "I bathed this morning. I only smell you, *Your Royal Highness*."

A growl slipped from Kai's lips at that vexatious title. "Now you test me on purpose."

Luca's mouth curved into a cocky grin. "My scent's made to prepare you for rutting." His omega tipped his head toward Kai's crotch. "Are you prepared, *Your Highness*?"

The shortened version of Kai's title wasn't much better. He let it go, since Luca was teasing him. Purposely pushing his buttons. And here he worried his fated mate wouldn't be a challenge, that he'd be too compliant.

Surprise, surprise.

This whole fated mate thing might work out much better than Kai originally thought.

The only lovers he'd ever had in the past that gave him any challenge, made him excited to do more than just rut, were... humans. The betas in the king's stable were too much of the "yes" type. They did what they were told, and that was it. There was usually no passion, no excitement. That's why for the past few years he'd turned to human males. They, at least, didn't give a flying fish that Kai was a prince. They weren't worried about royal politics. They just wanted to have fun and weren't afraid to do whatever they needed to do to make sure they, and Kai, got off.

However, being a Selkie alpha, Kai's cock was bigger than most and he had the ability to knot. He always had to take care when rutting with humans, so he didn't lose control and knot them, possibly severely injuring them in the process. Though a few had begged him for it.

And he had been tempted. Sorely tempted.

The only beings he knew who could comfortably take an alpha's knot was an omega. They were built for it, especially when in oestrus. So even when he rutted with betas he needed to be careful. Though he knew which betas at their disposal could take the knot and which couldn't. And sometimes Kai just felt like a nut... *err*, a knot.

He frowned.

He shouldn't be thinking about betas or even humans when he had a willing omega in his suite of rooms. He glanced at his watch again. They still had twenty minutes to go.

They needed to continue their small talk to hopefully pass the time more quickly. He should ask Luca about his family, his hobbies, his...

"Are you on any type of heat suppressant?" Kai groaned. What the hell was wrong with him?

Color flooded Luca's cheeks. Though Kai didn't think it was from embarrassment. "No. I was instructed to stop taking them a week ago."

Kai swallowed hard. He knew the first time he bred with Luca, his sperm could induce a heat cycle. And a heat cycle could produce a pregnancy. Which meant having an heir sooner than he expected. It also meant his fated mate's life would be at risk. He could lose Luca before he even got a good chance to know him.

The only way to avoid that would be to wear a condom and he wasn't about to do that. Not only were they frowned upon among the Selkie race, he couldn't knot his mate wearing one. Doing so would split it open and be ineffective, anyway.

And he so wanted to knot his omega.

Kai lifted his wrist and gritted his teeth. Eighteen minutes to go.

Then Vin entered the room and Kai sighed in relief until he saw Douglass flitting around right on Vin's heels.

Shit.

It was show time.

CHAPTER THREE

"I'm sorry," Kai yelled out as Luca rushed down the hall back toward his... *their* wing in the castle.

Holy Poseidon, that had been a horrible experience. Kai blamed himself for it. He should've paid attention when Douglass explained the traditions a couple of years ago once the Seekers were preparing to present potential omegas to him.

But he hadn't paid attention. For that, he was an idiot.

He should have bucked the tradition and refused to put him and Luca through that epically embarrassing ceremony. It was bad enough when Luca had to kneel naked and present his ass during the Presentation Ceremony earlier in the day, but that... that *ceremony* in the Great Hall tonight was so much bloody worse.

No wonder he wasn't allowed to be present at any of his father's bonding ceremonies when he was a small pup. The last one held was to Caol's *pater* and Kai had been only five at the time. He might have been scarred for life if he had witnessed it.

Douglass was lucky he wasn't within arm's reach right now, or Kai would strangle the flighty pest until he turned blue.

For whatever reason, Kai had thought that the Bonding Ceremony included both him and Luca putting on their seal skins then saying some words, maybe over a candle or something. And possibly going out for their first swim together as a bonded couple in the Great Sea.

But, oh, it was nothing romantic like that at all.

It certainly wasn't.

"Shit!" Kai screamed to the empty hallway, Luca long gone. He only hoped his omega truly escaped to their suites and didn't head out of the castle, out of the compound, hell, out of the colony never to be seen again.

It was while Kai watched in horror at the procedure that was being done to Luca when he realized he was now determined to take the throne and stop all these barbaric, old-fashioned traditions. That particular one would be the first thing to be disposed of on his agenda.

Had no one explained the Bonding Ceremony to Luca? Had he gone into it totally unaware of what would happen to him?

Kai's heart pounded as he moved faster down the hallway, passing the corridor that led to Caol's quarters. Then he started to jog, worried that his fated mate really would run away.

Kai wouldn't blame him one bit.

How could he have let this happen?

He ran down the corridor to the entrance to his quarters and opened the door. Or tried to. Did his omega lock him out?

He tried again, and, with a hard shove, the heavy wooden door finally opened. Relief flooded him. He'd have to get Vin to get the latch fixed. In his haste, Kai forgot that it sometimes stuck.

His gaze swept the large living quarters, then he peeked into the kitchen and his study, finding those rooms equally empty. He continued on, rushing up the stone stairs to his bedroom suite. "Luca!" he called.

His racing heart slowed to a dull thud when he received no answer.

Kai bounced a fist against his forehead with how stupid he had been. He swore he was never speaking to the king or his faithful suckerfish Douglass again. Never.

And he had been so close to punching his brother Rian in the face, too.

Kai hurried to his bedroom door and as he tried to open it, it didn't budge. He tried again. Now, he knew *this* door didn't stick. Luca had to have locked it. He jiggled the handle in frustration.

In one way, he was relieved that Luca hadn't run away and had come back to their quarters. In another, he was disturbed and a little annoyed that Luca locked him out. Especially since the omega could not deny his alpha ever.

"Luca," Kai called through the heavy door. Again, no answer. He leaned his forehead against the cool wood and repeated Luca's name louder this time. Nothing.

"Luca, you cannot deny me. You cannot lock me out. That's a punishable offense."

While it *was* a punishable offense, Kai would never report it. He'd just hoped the empty threat would get Luca to open the door, so he could tend to his hurting omega.

"Please, on the soul of the great Poseidon, *please* open the door."

Again, no answer.

"I'm not leaving. I'll stay right here until you let me in. I just want to see if you're all right."

More silence. Kai pressed his ear to the door. Unfortunately, it was so thick that anything heard through it would be muffled. But he swore he heard what sounded like soft weeping.

He closed his eyes and slid down the door to the floor. Leaning against it, he raised a hand to press his palm against the polished wood.

"I'm sorry. I'm sorry. I'm sorry," Kai repeated in a murmur. He raised his voice. "Luca, I'll be here waiting until whenever you're ready."

Kai dropped his hand, pulled his thighs to his chest, wrapped his arms around his legs and pressed his forehead to his knees. He was there for the duration. He would give Luca the time he needed since his omega deserved at least that. Kai only hoped it wasn't too long. Because if it was, Kai would have to pull his alpha rank on him and force his way into his own bedroom. Or at least get a key from Vin.

They should be inside his sleeping quarters together, consummating their bond at this very moment, not separated by a thick slab of wood and some cold stone walls.

He took a deep breath and closed his eyes, settling in for what could be a long wait.

Not twenty minutes later, Kai heard the latch on the other side of the door being unlocked. He waited, but the door remained closed.

With a groan, he pushed himself to his feet, rubbing away his stiffness. The stone had robbed his muscles of their warmth and sitting on a floor was not the most comfortable.

But then neither was what Luca had been forced to endure.

He put his hand on the handle, took another deep breath to brace himself, then opened the door.

The room was dark except for the fire that burned in the hearth, giving the room a soft glow. As his eyes adjusted slightly, he scanned the room, his gaze landing on a dark figure on his bed. "Can I turn on the lights?"

When he received no answer, Kai flipped the switch, the electric lanterns that dotted the walls lit up, allowing him to see Luca curled up into a ball in the center of his large bed.

Kai's lips flattened, but he held back from rushing over to inspect his omega.

"Luca," he said gently. "May I join you?"

He didn't have to ask, but he wanted to. Even though Luca might be an omega, he was still a living being. One with feelings and one who could be hurt. Luca was his to take care of, so he needed to do just that.

When he heard a muffled noise come from the bed, he took that as a yes and moved forward, stopping when he reached the side of the king-sized bed. His omega's face was turned away, so Kai reached out and brushed a hand over Luca's dark blond hair, which was on the longish side. It was thick, soft and silky between his fingers. His omega had a beautiful head of hair to match his stunning sea green eyes.

"Luca," he whispered and settled on the edge of the bed, the thick mattress sinking beneath his weight. "Please talk to me." Kai rubbed his hand up and down Luca's back in an attempt to soothe him.

His mate's breath hitched and then he said shakily, "I'm sorry, my prince, I could not..."

My prince. Kai bit back a sigh. That title was the least of his worries right now. "Could not what?" he encouraged Luca to continue.

"Could not be brave enough..."

Kai's spine straightened. "Brave enough? That had nothing to do with bravery or lack thereof."

Luca suddenly pushed up and turned to face him.

Kai reached out to brush a tear off his omega's pale cheek with his thumb. "I can't tell you enough how sorry I am. I—"

Luca cut him off, his face becoming flush. "I already had a medical exam before the Seekers would even consider presenting me. It was required. I don't understand why... *they*... had to do it that way."

Kai's jaw tightened at the hurt in Luca's voice. *They.* The "chosen" Selkies that the Royal Council appointed to lead and partake in these bonding ceremonies. They had been introduced at the start of the ceremony and Kai would never forget their names. *Ever.* "Traditions," he spat out.

Luca's voice was raw when he continued, "When you said you'd 'mark' me, I thought you meant with your scent when we..."

"I did. I had no idea—"

"They *branded* me!" Luca cried out and shivered, his hand automatically going to his ass cheek where he'd been branded with a red-hot iron.

A branding iron made in the shape of the king's insignia. The awful smell of burning flesh was still stuck in Kai's throat and nostrils.

Kai grabbed Luca's hand, pulling it away from his buttocks, and held it tightly in his lap, brushing a thumb over Luca's knuckles. "I know. I'm sorry. I... I could say I didn't know, but that's no excuse because I was probably told, and just didn't care at the time. I really didn't care if my fated mate was ever found since it wasn't important to me. I was foolish and this is all my fault. Again, I can't say it enough... I'm sorry, Luca."

As if Kai hadn't spoken, Luca continued, his voice higher-pitched than normal. "Then they wanted us to rut in front of *everyone.*"

Kai squeezed his eyes shut. That was the point where Kai disrupted the whole ceremony, pulling Luca off the platform and demanding he put his clothes back on. He firmly, and in no uncertain terms, had told his father they were done, that the ceremony was over, and they were going back to their wing to finish the bonding ceremony in private. That the king, his brothers and the other nobility that were invited as witnesses would have to take his word that the bonding would be completed, but not in front of their eyes.

Hell no, it wouldn't be. He was not going to mate with his omega on a raised platform surrounded by other males watching. Especially his own family.

A shudder went through him.

A knock on his bedroom door made his eyes narrow as his head swung in that direction. Who in Hades would dare interrupt them at this moment?

He reluctantly released his mate's hand and with long strides, Kai rushed over to jerk the door open. Vin bowed slightly, his eyes downcast, as he held up a glass mason jar of what looked like water.

His beta servant's subservient attitude surprised him because it was so unlike Vin.

"Prince Kai, I've... I've brought this. The sea water will help speed up the healing. Unless... unless you would like me to escort you both to the cave to get your skins and go for a swim? I promise it will help soothe the burn."

Kai glanced over his shoulder to where Luca now stood at a window, his back to them as he stared out into the dark of the night, his arms wrapped around his waist. There was a curve to his omega's shoulders that made Kai's chest ache.

"Luca, are you up for a swim? Did you hear Vin?"

"I don't want to run into anybody. I can't face anyone... tonight."

His voice was thin and sounded so frail. Nothing like his obstinate, plucky omega earlier. His spirit seemed to have fled.

Kai wanted to punch a wall.

He turned back to Vin, who still had his head bowed since he could not only sense Kai's extreme anger but could most likely smell it. It had to permeate from Kai's pores.

Kai removed the jar from Vin's white-knuckled fingers. He'd never seen his personal servant so nervous before and the beta normally didn't call him Prince either. The news of Kai's fury must have moved like lightning through the castle.

"Thank you, Vin. You may leave us."

With his head still down, Vin bowed just slightly at the waist. "Yes, Prince Kai. Please summon me if you need anything else tonight. Otherwise, I'll be here first thing in the morning to prepare a meal to break the fast."

With a nod, Kai lowered his voice until only his beta servant could hear him. "Make it extra special, please. And do not let anyone else in to share it with us. It's important that we break our fast in private tomorrow. Understood?"

Vin tilted his head barely enough for Kai to see it. "I do, sir." With that, his loyal servant turned on his heels, and Kai shut the door. He stared at it for a moment, trying to cool his temper, before turning to study Luca across the room.

The reflection of his omega's face in the window showed that his mate was devastated and felt deceived. And seeing that shattered Kai as well.

He took the jar of sea water and placed it by the bed, then moved to stand behind Luca, both of their reflections now clear in the window. Kai dark and tall, Luca light, more slight of body and a bit shorter. Admittedly, they made a good match as their looks complimented each other and they would make very handsome pups.

That was *if* his omega could ever forgive him and move past this horrible experience. They needed to finish the bonding, and they needed to do it soon. Without being bonded, the king could get a hair up his ass about Luca and him not finishing the ceremony and send his omega away as punishment, fated mate or not.

Unfortunately, his father's word was the law in this colony and the Royal Guards would obey any command he gave them. Not to mention, the little rat Douglass would just love the opportunity to make sure Kai suffered in some way.

Kai lifted his hands to place them on Luca's shoulders, but the omega ducked away before he could touch him.

He turned to watch Luca cross the bedroom, then spin on his heels to face Kai, his face a tortured mask.

"After the exam... when it was announced that I wasn't a virgin..."

Both Kai's jaw and chest got tight. He didn't care one whit that Luca's corona membrane had not been intact. There was nothing illegal about Luca coming to him no longer a virgin. While there was nothing in the Royal Council's scrolls, either, that required an omega to be a virgin in order to become a mate of nobility, it was preferred. And since Kai was a prince, he could cast aside Luca for a virgin mate, fated or not.

"When they asked you if you wanted to ignore the fates and find someone pure and intact..."

Kai's nostrils flared.

"You didn't answer them," Luca finished in a whisper.

No, he didn't. Kai tried to force down the lump in his throat, not sure if he wanted to know the answer to a question he needed to ask, one thing he *needed* to know... "Have you rutted with another alpha?"

Luca turned away before saying, "I was on heat suppressants."

That wasn't an answer.

Blood rushed into Kai's ears. "Luca, look at me. Have you rutted with another alpha?"

Luca's silence was Kai's answer.

Omegas were never to rut with alphas. Not unless they were their mates. Betas were more acceptable because there was no fear of an omega getting pregnant with a beta. But the risk was there with an alpha. There was also a risk of unintended bonding.

Kai started to step forward, to grab his omega and shake some sense into him, but he stopped himself. "Why? If it had to be someone, why not a beta?"

Luca avoided his gaze. "I was young. I foolishly wanted to experience a... a knot." The last two words came out as a broken whisper.

Kai closed his eyes for a moment, not sure if he wanted to hear the answer to his next question. "And did this alpha knot you?"

After a couple heartbeats, Luca finally answered. "Yes."

Kai shouldn't ask the next question, either. "Did you like it?"

Luca's answer came much quicker this time. "I did. Very much."

Kai fought down the rush of jealousy that bubbled up from his gut. Another alpha had knotted his fated mate. Another alpha had not only taken his omega's virginity but had given Luca pleasure. And his omega hadn't been forced. No, he had wanted it. He had wanted to be knotted even though it was forbidden.

This knowledge should change everything.

"Simply not being a virgin gives me enough cause to cast you aside, Luca, and find a new mate. Are you aware of that? But... having an alpha, who is not your mate, knot you is..."

"Against the law."

Against the law. "Did the Seekers not ask if you were a virgin?"

"They did."

"And you lied?"

"No. I told them I wasn't. But they didn't ask if I'd ever been knotted. Or even to whom I lost my virginity."

They must have assumed it had been to a beta, so of course they wouldn't have asked if he'd been knotted.

"And if they would have, Luca? Would you have lied?"

Luca continued to stare at the floor at his feet. "Yes. I wouldn't have wanted to bring shame upon my family. My father

THE SELKIE PRINCE'S FATED MATE   37

and my *pater*, they're good people from good bloodlines. I couldn't do that to them."

"Do you regret it?"

Kai couldn't miss the deep inhale Luca took as he raised his gaze to Kai and met his eyes directly. Kai's heart thumped heavily against his chest at Luca's next answer.

"I didn't."

"But now?"

"Now I do."

"Why? Because you could be cast aside?"

Luca shook his head. "No."

"Then what?"

"Because I regret not giving you, my alpha bull, the gift of my virginity. It was meant for my fated mate and no one else. And for that, I am sorry. I hope you can forgive me, my prince."

All the oxygen fled Kai's lungs. He blinked, trying to absorb everything Luca had just said. While he couldn't understand why Luca would desire to be knotted by an alpha other than his mate, he could understand how bad decisions can be made. Luca's life and his family's reputation could be ruined by his selfish desire. Understandably, all males had them. Maybe they all didn't act on them, or maybe they weren't brought to light in this fashion, so they got away with them at the very least.

The mates of nobility, especially of kings and princes, tended to be held to a higher standard. This was why the Selkies who examined Luca during the ceremony asked if Kai would rather accept another omega who was "pure."

A standard Kai didn't give a flying fish about.

But Luca accepting the knot from another alpha, and most likely encouraging it, surprised him. And admittedly, bothered him. There was a purpose behind the knot and while it was pleasurable for the alpha and usually for the omega, as well, it wasn't meant to be done strictly for pleasure. It was to ensure pregnancy.

Some omegas could get heady during a knot, whether in oestrus or not. Some loved it like a sexual kink. He wondered if Luca was that way. It would be interesting to see if his mate demanded his knot often. Would it bother Kai if it turned out that Luca was like that?

Again, Kai could give a rat's ass when it came to normal standards. He himself liked a little rough play when he rutted. If knotting brought Luca pleasure than why would Kai deny him?

"I will make you a deal, Luca, my bringer of light. I will forgive you for your youthful mistake if you will forgive me for not paying attention when I should have... for not caring enough to know in advance what would happen tonight. That was *my* youthful mistake. One I will not make again. I promise."

"So you won't cast me aside? You won't report me?"

Kai shook his head. "I will not. You're mine, Luca. You are my mate; the fates have decided that. And as such, we need to complete this bonding ceremony."

Luca's body went solid at Kai's words.

"Don't worry. I don't mean back in the Great Hall. I mean here in private. Just me and you."

His omega relaxed slightly, his shoulders lowering a touch. "Will that be enough? Will that be acceptable? To the king? To the Royal Council?"

"It will have to be."

"And if it isn't?"

"It will be," Kai promised, hoping that was true. "I've never said 'I'm sorry' more than tonight but I'm going to say it again. I'm sorry, Luca, but we must mate tonight. I know what you went through was appalling and I realize you might not be up for it, but we have no choice. I need to mark you with my scent and my seed, otherwise the king or even the Royal Council could take you away." When Luca didn't respond, Kai continued, "I was hoping this evening would have been more pleasant, and it's certainly not going how I thought it would, but—"

"Okay."

Kai tilted his head as he stared at Luca. "Okay?"

Luca nodded. "Yes, I understand the need for it. And I'm willing."

CHAPTER FOUR

"I WANT TO RUT WITH YOU," Luca continued, as he studied his alpha before him.

Kai's turquoise blue eyes darkened. "Are you sure?"

"Yes, I want you to take me and make me your bonded mate. I belong with you."

This day had been such a roller coaster of emotions but through all of it, Luca knew that was true. The fates were never wrong. He belonged to this alpha. He was destined to produce this prince's heirs.

Suddenly, the prince was moving toward him with a determined stride. Luca's eyes widened when the alpha never slowed, and they collided, the oxygen rushing from his lungs and before he could gasp, his alpha claimed his mouth.

Luca groaned and melted against the taller, stronger male when Kai's arms held Luca tightly against him. And, like magic, everything that happened earlier faded away. All his focus landed on his mate, his alpha, his Selkie prince, who was kissing him so thoroughly that his knees began to buckle.

Breaking the kiss, Kai swept him up into his arms and carried him to the bed, gently placing him onto the mattress.

"I need you to get undressed, Luca. Quickly."

His alpha's voice was noticeably strained, as were his pants. Kai's cock pressed against the fabric, making Luca lick his lips. He couldn't wait to taste his alpha's seed, but not this first time, no. This time was solely to bond them together as fated mates. It was important that Luca accept all of his mate's seed deep inside him. It would get his hormones ready for heat.

And once he went into heat...

Luca closed his eyes for a moment as he imagined falling into that uncontrollable desire during heat to mate repeatedly until his alpha's seed took root and he became pregnant.

But right now, he wasn't in heat. Though, that didn't mean he wouldn't enjoy rutting this alpha. The one who was stripping off his clothes as Luca just laid on the bed still fully dressed.

"Luca, hurry," Kai urged, pushing both his pants and boxers down his long, muscular legs in one swoop.

Luca sucked in a breath when he finally saw just how large and thick his alpha's cock was. Alpha's were larger than omegas and betas and, from what he'd heard, humans, so Kai's was nothing out of the ordinary. But still... It had been a while since the last time Luca had rutted.

"But I want to watch you," Luca began.

"You can stare at me afterward," Kai answered impatiently. "Right now, I can't wait. I can smell your slick."

Yes, Luca was leaking like a faucet. How could he not when Kai was so impressive? Not just his cock, but his lean, muscular structure, as well.

"Luca," Kai growled.

"I should make you undress me, my alpha bull," Luca teased.

Bull certainly was the right nickname for his mate.

Kai placed one knee on the edge of the bed, and grasping his cock in the other, he began to stroke it, making the slick leak from Luca's hole even faster. "If I undress you, Omega, your clothes will end up shredded. Do not delay."

Luca rose to his knees in the middle of the bed, reaching for the top button of his dress shirt. "So I shouldn't take my time and tease you?"

"Not if you like those clothes you're wearing," Kai growled, sending a shiver down Luca's spine to land in his ass.

His hole twitched, and his sphincter loosened. "I'm soaking these pants, anyway."

Kai blew out a breath and squeezed the head of his cock so hard it turned purple.

Luca's fingers trembled as he hurried to slide the buttons through their holes.

"Faster," Kai demanded, his hand stroking his cock even more rapidly.

Luca licked his lips when he spotted the precum beading at the tip and said, "Can I just—?"

"No!" Kai barked then blew out a breath. "Please, I can't... Just hurry."

Luca quickly finished unbuttoning his shirt, slipped it off his shoulders and tossed it over the side of the bed. He had removed his shoes earlier before curling up in Kai's bed, so he yanked off his socks and unzipped his dress pants before carefully shimmying out of them with barely a wince of pain from the fresh brand.

"Boxers, too," his impatient prince ordered.

With a small smile, Luca gingerly worked those down to reveal just how hard he was, as well. Though his cock wasn't lacking, it was nowhere near his alpha's size. He squeezed his ass cheeks together because his anus was now throbbing, and arousal was starting to drip down his crease and his thighs.

"You smell ready... *so* good. It's like a drug," Kai murmured.

"How do you want me?"

"In so many ways."

A smile tugged at Luca's mouth. "But right now?"

"Right now, I just need to... I promise we'll take our time later..."

Luca understood completely. It wasn't just getting the mating over with for bonding purposes, but the scent of one's fated mate could be heady. It made breeding easier for a new couple, especially if they didn't know each other beforehand, because the prince was right, the scent was like a drug and quite irresistible.

"I'll get into position, then," Luca stated as he moved to his hands and knees, his heart racing with anticipation.

The bed dipped from the prince's weight and Luca couldn't resist turning to glance over his shoulder at him. And because he was watching, Luca shouldn't have jerked in surprise when Kai touched his anus, sliding a finger through the slippery arousal that was escaping.

"Luca, you please me." The prince lifted his hand showing Luca how shiny with slick his fingers were, then rubbed the natural lubricant over his cock. Kai did it several more times until his cock was as shiny as his fingers. Then those fingers were back, sliding along his crease, dipping inside him, making a groan escape Luca.

As Kai worked his fingers in and out, he said tightly, "I'll try to be gentle, Luca. But if I'm not..."

Luca gathered his wits enough to say, "No, no apologies. You've done that enough already tonight."

"Please feel free to tell me to slow down or not be so rough. I don't want to hurt you."

As long as Kai didn't touch the fresh brand which was at the top of Luca's right ass cheek... "You won't."

Luca didn't want to admit to his mate that he not only lost his virginity to the alpha who knotted him, but he'd met that alpha many times in secret. His alpha lover was never gentle during their rutting and knotted him every time. Luca had loved and begged for every bit of it. But he and that alpha had no feelings for one another and once Luca was destined to be presented by the Seekers to nobility, he broke off their affair much to the alpha's dismay.

Luca swallowed hard as Kai shifted closer. In just a few more seconds, he was about to become the bonded mate of a prince.

"Like I said, we'll take our time to explore each other, to get to know each other better later."

"So you're just doing this for my own good?" Luca teased.

"No... I'm doing this because I can't resist you." And with that, Kai moved forward and pressed his cock slowly inside him.

With a groan, Luca pushed his hips back, taking his alpha's whole length, feeling it fill him completely. It didn't hurt at all; his body easily accommodated the alpha's size as if they were made for each other.

But before he could savor the fullness, Kai was moving hard and fast, gripping Luca's hips so tightly his fingers dug into Luca's flesh, but still carefully avoiding the area where the symbol had been seared into his skin. The slapping of their skin together made Luca bite his bottom lip and his eyes roll back.

There was nothing romantic about this private bonding ceremony, either. It was pure animalistic need. Kai was right. He was rough, slamming his cock deep, pulling out and slamming it again, while grunting with each stroke.

Even so, Luca cried out with how good it all felt. He didn't mind it rough and quick as long as they could take their time later as the prince promised. And, of course, there was one other thing he deeply desired.

"That's it, my bull, will you knot me?"

When Kai's cock grew even larger as it engorged with blood in preparation for knotting, Luca panted with anticipation.

"I need you to knot me," Luca encouraged, frustrated that his alpha had not said if he would do so tonight. He should have asked prior to the prince taking him. An alpha could control the knot when an omega was not in heat. When they were in heat, he lost that control completely.

"My alpha bull, please... *please* knot me."

Kai's thrusting slowed, and he curled over Luca's back, his palms planting into the mattress next to Luca's, then his mouth was at the back of Luca's neck.

"I will knot you, my mate. I'll fill you with my seed. I'll do whatever you'd like, Luca, to make you mine. Whatever you want from me, I'll give you."

Luca moaned at his intoxicating words. "I want your knot and your mark."

"And you shall have it."

Luca cried out as Kai bit the back of his neck and held his flesh between his teeth tightly. His alpha's cock thickened deep inside him, the bulbus glandis at the root swelling large enough to tie them together. Luca's body automatically responded when his sphincter tightened around it, completing the lock.

Kai sank his teeth more firmly into Luca's neck as he came deep inside him, the strong pulses filling Luca up with his seed. This rutting could induce a heat cycle which would cause more frantic rutting than what they just did. Though, Luca hoped that his heat would hold off for a few days or even a few weeks until Luca and Kai got to know each other better both in and out of bed.

Kai finally released his hold on the back of his neck, but brushed kisses along Luca's skin where he was sure a mark was left. Then, after his alpha laid a line of kisses down Luca's spine, Kai finally rose up. It would be five minutes, if not more, before the swelling of the knot and the blood flow to Kai's cock lessened enough to be able to separate.

But in the meantime, they needed to get comfortable. However, it was hard to relax when Luca still had a raging erection of his own. He reached between his legs and jerked at it roughly, but Kai stopped him with a sharp, "No," as if he was scolding Luca.

"Let me take care of you," he said more softly. "Let's lower to our sides."

Carefully, Kai directed them until they lay on their sides, Kai spooning Luca's back. His alpha buried his face into Luca's neck but this time he didn't use his teeth. He was much more gentle as he nuzzled Luca's scent gland with his nose, taking deep long inhales. Kai reached around Luca and trailed his long fingers along Luca's thigh and up to his sac where he cupped it and squeezed just slightly. Then wrapping his fingers around Luca's length, he began to stroke.

With his alpha still knotted deep inside him and his hand on Luca's cock, it didn't take long for Luca to lose himself once again. Kai kept Luca's legs pinned to the bed with one of his own, so Luca wouldn't thrust into Kai's hand, hurting himself in the process by pulling against the knot. Instead, Kai did all the work, stroking and squeezing, thumbing the beads of precum from the swollen head until Luca was panting and whimpering, shoving his head back into Kai's collar bone as his alpha whispered encouraging words into his ear.

Within minutes, Luca's hot cum was spurting furiously, landing on his belly and chest as he came with an intensity he never had before. When he was done, he felt drained, but satisfied.

Especially when his fated mate growled the following words into his ear, "No other alpha will have you again, Luca. None. You're mine. No one will dare touch you now that you carry my scent. And you belong to me."

CHAPTER FIVE

IN THE GLOW of the fire, Kai studied his fated—and now bonded —mate as Luca slept soundly. He was pleased that his omega could sleep after everything that happened the day before. But then, Luca had been exhausted, not only from the mental drain of two embarrassing ceremonies but from them rutting three times throughout the night. The first time had been rushed until they knotted. But the next two times, they mated at a slower pace, exploring each other and learning each other's bodies and their sexual preferences. But they were clearly not done doing so, as they had so much more to learn. He was pleased that Luca didn't mind being taken roughly and his omega, in fact, encouraged it. But now his mind wandered to whether Luca's former alpha lover had been just as rough. He tamped down the jealousy as best as he could.

Each time they rutted last night, Luca begged for his knot. *Every time.* Confirming Kai's suspicions that the omega considered knotting an erotic gratification, not just a means to become pregnant. Luca did not complain once of it being too painful or of him being sore. And as long as Kai was capable of giving Luca what he wanted, he'd do so. Seeing his mate in ecstasy gave Kai unexpected satisfaction.

However, each time the knot lasted longer due to Kai becoming weary. And the final time, it lasted a good twenty minutes. Or at least that's what Kai assumed, because both of them had drifted off while still tied together. Eventually, Kai had woken to find them untied, and he had gone into the bathroom to clean up while Luca continued to sleep.

He would need to have Vin bring fresh sheets since the bed was a complete mess from his omega's generous amount of slick and Luca's cum that shot in hot, ropey spurts all over them both, as well as the bed.

Kai had to admit it was not pleasant to sleep in that damp mess all night. He would need to find a solution. Or maybe Vin already knew of one. If his bed ended up in such a state with just three rounds of rutting, he couldn't imagine how it would be once his omega went into oestrus. During the heat cycle, the rutting was endless. As soon as they would unlock, Kai knew he'd be driven again to rut and knot his omega. It was an instinct that remained from the past when Selkies were more seal than human. By being constantly tied to their mate during oestrus, it reduced the risk of another alpha coming along and mating with the omega, possibly being the one to impregnate the fertile male. Or female, since female Selkies did exist until about three hundred years ago.

With all his former lovers, Kai had simply done the deed and then left the beta's quarters—or the human's home—immediately afterward, not worrying about any mess left behind. Though some of his male human lovers had begged him to stay the night, he never did. Visit them, yes. Stay the whole night, no. Humans tended to get attached too easily.

Because the top sheet of the bed had ended up in a tangled mess, they had slept without it. Between the fire in the hearth

THE SELKIE PRINCE'S FATED MATE   51

and the heat of each other's bodies as they embraced, they had remained plenty warm during the cold early winter night. But now, Kai laid on his side as his omega slept on his belly, snoring softly.

His lips curled up at the corners as he gazed along the trim body of his mate. Luca's skin was smooth and pale, no mark or mole to be found. His fingers and toes were slightly webbed like Kai's. Not enough to draw the attention of a human from a distance, but up close, yes, it was easy to tell. It was a telltale sign of being a Selkie. Kai traced his fingertips along the curve of Luca's spine until he reached his rump, which was as enticing as his scent. He frowned as he studied the brand that now marred his omega's perfect skin.

Anger bubbled up once more, and he closed his eyes as he relived the scene from last night. He would never forget the smell or even the horrifying sounds that Luca made while the glowing, hot iron had been pressed into his flesh.

Reaching over his mate, Kai grabbed the jar of sea water and twisted open the metal lid. He dipped two fingers inside and then lightly applied the sea water to the brand. He had done it several times throughout the night and each time the brand healed a little more. Being Selkie shifters, they healed faster than humans. But Vin was probably right about taking Luca out for a swim. If they had donned their skins and went out into the Great Sea, it might have been healed by now. The only thing remaining would be a raised scar in the shape of the King of the North's insignia, marking Luca forever as Kai's.

Maybe after breakfast, Kai could convince Luca to go down to the cave to don their skins and they could not only enjoy their first swim together as a bonded couple, but finish healing that wound.

Brushing his wet fingers over his omega's ass was starting to send the blood rushing to his cock. He must have gotten enough sleep between their rutting to recharge his batteries. He was dying to take Luca while he was on his back, but until the brand was completely healed, he couldn't. He wouldn't cause his omega that pain for his own selfish desires.

"You didn't get enough, my bull?" Luca asked, his voice thick with sleep.

"I was just applying more sea water to your brand," Kai said with feigned innocence.

Luca shifted and twisted his head enough on the pillow to run his gaze along Kai's naked body. "And does tending to another medically always get you ready to rut?"

Kai chuckled. "I've never done it before, honestly. That's what betas are for. However, it's not my caring for you that's making me hard, it's how beautiful your ass is." Kai leaned closer and pressed his nose to Luca's scent gland. "And how perfect you smell now that your scent is combined with your alpha's."

"You like to smell yourself?" Luca teased.

"I like that you smell of me." Kai traced Luca's ear with the tip of his tongue. "And now I need you to give me your mouth, so I can give you a thorough 'good morning' kiss."

"Mmm. Have you never done that before, either?" Luca teased some more.

Kai hesitated. Actually, he hadn't. Again, when he rutted he only did it with either a beta kept for that purpose or a human. He'd never actually slept beside anyone all night or woke up next to a lover in the morning. Amazingly, he didn't mind sharing his bed all night with his newly bonded mate. In fact, he now couldn't imagine not sleeping beside him.

Instead of answering Luca, Kai captured his lips and kissed him deeply, exploring every recess of his mouth until his omega groaned and squirmed against him. Kai pulled away just slightly. "Are you now as ready to rut as I am?"

"Hmm. After one more kiss maybe."

Kai obliged, giving his omega what he wanted, taking his time and not breaking the kiss until he was swallowing Luca's moans and groans. Quickly releasing him, Kai rolled up and over him until he straddled the back Luca's legs, pinning him to the bed.

"Show me how wet you are, my mate."

With an impatient noise, Luca reached back and spread his ass cheeks, showing Kai just what he expected. His puckered hole was loose and slick, ready to receive Kai's cock.

But Kai wasn't ready to give it to him. Instead, he leaned over and brushed his lips over the spot on the back of Luca's neck which still held the mark where Kai bit him each time they'd rutted during the night. The instinct to bite Luca's neck when he knotted was so strong that he was glad that Luca didn't mind it. That instinct also went back hundreds of years to when their DNA was more seal than human. By holding his mate down by the back of the neck until they were securely locked together ensured neither would be injured in the process.

Because spraining his cock while trying to tie his mate was not on his to-do list anytime soon.

He continued to kiss along Luca's shoulders and down his spine until he reached the top of his cleft. The overwhelming scent of his Omega's slick spurred him to take him immediately. But he didn't. He wanted to pleasure his mate in a new way this morning.

Sliding down Luca's legs, Kai brushed his mate's hands away and spread his buttocks apart himself.

"You're open for me."

Luca made a noise into the pillow that could have been a yes, but it didn't matter. The amount of slick that Luca was producing was proof enough that he was ready and wanting this as much as Kai.

He slid his tongue down his crease until he circled Luca's hole, savoring the taste of Luca's arousal on his tongue. He circled the omega's entrance a couple times and when Luca groaned loudly, he did it some more.

With a smile, he pulled away and said, "You taste as good as you smell."

Before he could shift forward to give Luca his cock, Kai heard a distant, muffled noise. He tilted his head and listened more carefully.

Luca lifted his head. "Is something wrong?"

"Sounds like Vin is here making our morning meal."

"Are you not going to make me yours then, my bull?"

"Oh no, I'm taking you," Kai answered. "We just won't have time to knot."

"You can knot me tonight."

"You're insatiable."

"I am, my bull, for your seed. So please hurry and give your omega what he needs."

Kai snorted. "Did you mean to rhyme?"

Luca chuckled into the pillow. "No, but I may have to start writing some poems for us to recite during our rutting."

"Just what I wanted in a mate, one who writes poetry and sings sonnets," Kai said dryly.

"As you wish. I will start on that soon after my bull has had his way with me."

"*Ah*, then I better hurry."

"Yes, please do."

With a smile, Kai settled over Luca, rubbing the engorged head of his cock back and forth over his slick hole, gathering the natural lubricant. "Are you ready to start singing?"

Luca's body shook with laughter beneath him. But it quickly stilled and his hips tilted up as Kai drove his cock deep with a sigh.

Being inside his omega was like nothing he could describe clearly. It was a mixture of joy and comfort, warmth and love all wrapped into the simple act of rutting. But it wasn't just that. Rutting was what he did with his former lovers. With Luca it was more like sharing, mating and bonding. A connection that only got stronger each time they were together. It was almost as if Kai had found a missing piece of himself.

Every time he was inside Luca, he felt whole.

Luca was his forever mate. He was born to be with Kai. The fates had seen to it. And they were never wrong.

Kai reached under Luca, found his erection and fisted it. With every pump of his hips against his mate's ass, Kai pumped Luca's cock with his hand.

Luca belonged to him. Belonged *with* him.

If the Seekers had not found Luca, Kai would still be missing a piece of himself and he wouldn't have even been aware that part of him was absent. He couldn't believe he never cared if the Seekers ever found his mate. Once he'd become old enough to rut, he was fine with doing it with whoever was willing. He thought living that way, in that mindset, for the rest of his life would be sufficient.

But now after one night with his fated mate, everything had changed. There was now a meaning to the act, an actual emotional connection. It should scare him, this sudden change, this pressing need to be with this male he hardly knew. But it didn't. His heart seemed to swell within his chest a little more each time he made Luca his, every time he planted his seed deep within his mate.

Luca, Kai's bringer of light.

The fates knew exactly what they were doing.

With a grunt, he thrust harder and faster and Luca clenched tightly around him and moaned, a move Kai was quickly recognizing as something Luca would do to encourage Kai to knot him. But like he had said, they didn't have time for that this morning.

They needed food in their bellies, and Kai needed to take

Luca for a long, healing swim and after that, who knew what the day would bring. He was sure at some point he would need to answer to his father.

He pushed that dread away and concentrated on the here and now and his beautiful omega beneath him. He should only be having pleasant thoughts while being buried deep within his mate's ass.

Luca squirmed. "Please knot me, my bull."

"We can't, Luca. I explained why."

"Vin can wait another ten minutes."

"It's not going to be ten minutes. We both need to shower this sticky mess off us."

"I can live with the mess if you can. And maybe the knot will only last for five."

Kai blew out a breath. Why did his mate tempt him so?

"Please, my bull, give me your knot."

Luca was quickly learning how to manipulate Kai. And even though Kai was quite aware of what his omega was doing, he still found Luca hard to resist. At least at this point. Maybe once they were an old mated couple, he'd be able to ignore Luca's begging and wouldn't give into his omega's demands so easily.

But for now...

Kai groaned as Luca wiggled his hips and clenched down around Kai's cock once again. He tried to fight the knot, but it was a struggle he was quickly losing.

"Luca..."

"Please, my prince, give me your knot and your seed."

Bloody hell. Kai squeezed his eyes shut when he couldn't control the blood rushing into his cock, making it swell even further, then his knot popped, and Luca cried out in pleasure as his tight ring held Kai fast.

Kai grunted as his balls pulled tight and his cum spurted in strong, steady streams deep inside his mate.

"Yesss," Luca hissed in what sounded like ecstasy and then came in Kai's fist.

After a few moments, once their breathing slowed, they moved to a more comfortable position in their wait to untie and Luca whispered, "Thank you, my bull."

Kai sighed and pressed a kiss into his hair. "You're welcome, Luca."

Kai was turning into a weak sap. He reached between his legs to make sure his balls were still intact because he could have sworn he'd lost them along the way.

———

AFTER EATING the delicious breakfast Vin prepared, the beta escorted them out of the castle, making sure no one saw them leave. Luca still wasn't ready to face anyone, not after that horrendous bonding ceremony last night.

And he certainly wasn't ready to speak with King Solomon, even though the male was now the equivalent of his "father-in-law." By Selkie law, anyway. The humans had their own laws and traditions when it came to bonding. Marriage was what they called it. And they also had divorce, a process that did not exist in the Selkie race.

For a Selkie to get rid of one's mate, they needed to be either banished or, more simply, cast aside. Luca knew that banishment was much more devastating than just a document claiming a couple was divorced. Divorced humans were not chased out of their community or forbidden to interact with their race. Banished Selkies were not only sent out of a colony and prohibited from returning, they couldn't be taken in by any other colony, either. To take in an exiled Selkie, one could face imprisonment or even death. Though, being executed for breaking the law hasn't happened in over a hundred years. Even so, that punishment was still valid in the scrolls of the Royal Council.

Luca had heard of a banished Selkie or two taking their own life because they couldn't bear to live without their family, their fated mate or their pups. He couldn't imagine the devastation a *pater* would endure by being banned from seeing a pup that he whelped. During the nine months of gestation, the *pater* developed an unbreakable bond with his son. The only time that it was severed was when the *pater* died in whelp or shortly thereafter.

Humans gave birth all the time and never died in childbirth anymore. Or at least it was rare. Luca couldn't understand why it wasn't the same with Selkies. Especially since they had access to the same modern medical treatments as humans did.

Hundreds of years ago only female Selkies carried the young and whelped them. Then they all began to die during whelp. As the race risked extinction, the males, who were a stronger sex, began to develop a way to take over the whelping. But by then, the last of the females had perished, leaving the males the only gender to remain. But not every male was able to bear pups. Only the omegas developed the womb needed to carry a pup since betas were infertile and alphas were the seed bearers. Luca didn't quite understand the genetics of it all, but he didn't know any different since this evolution occurred over a period of decades and that was hundreds of years ago.

All he needed to know was that an alpha could impregnate him during oestrus. Whether it be his bonded mate or another. And if an omega went into heat while he was not bonded, any alpha would be tempted to take him, and an omega usually would not resist due to the driving need to breed during that cycle. Any unplanned pup born to an unbonded omega would bring shame upon the omega's family. Omega's had been known to terminate unplanned pregnancies to save face within the community. While doing so was frowned upon and actually illegal, an omega who whelped a pup to an alpha who was not his mate lost all chance of being accepted by the alpha who should be his mate. Or the mate the fates deemed as such.

So bastard pups needed to be avoided at all costs.

But now, Luca didn't have to worry about all that. Any pups he whelped would belong to the alpha by his side as they currently followed his beta servant over a rocky terrain as they headed toward the Great Sea.

Luca's nostrils flared at the scent of salt water in the brisk air. It was intoxicating, and he couldn't wait to don his skin and take a dip in the frigid surf. He hoped the swim would reinvigorate him, push away his exhaustion from all the rutting last night, and finally complete the healing of the brand.

Tonight when he rutted with his prince, he wanted to be face to face with him. And preferred to do that while on his back. He wanted to watch his virile alpha bull take his ass and fill him full of his seed.

Luca shuddered with the anticipation of his alpha rutting him again and his cock twitched in his pants.

"Everything all right?" Kai asked him, concern in his Caribbean blue eyes as they walked side by side down a slope toward a rocky edge high above the sea.

"Yes, I was just imagining..." Luca let his words drift off since Vin was only a few feet in front of them.

"What I'll do to you tonight once that brand is healed?" Kai asked, a twinkle lighting up his eyes.

Luca shot Vin a quick glance before answering, "Yes."

Kai stopped abruptly, putting a hand on Luca's arm to halt his forward motion, as well. "Don't worry about what you say in front of Vin. He's been my faithful servant for a long time. In fact, since I was a young pup. He has selective hearing for a reason. And, don't forget, he was the one who had to change the sheets this morning. There was no hiding how active we were all night."

Heat rose up into Luca's cheeks.

Kai continued, "There's nothing you can say that would shock Vin, I promise. And I also trust him completely. If you need anything, Vin's your male. Just don't abuse him and he'll be faithful to you just as much as he is to me."

"I would never—"

"Yes, I know you wouldn't. I'm just, saying... He might be a beta servant but to me he's also family. Understood?"

Luca bowed his head. "Yes, my prince."

Kai turned Luca toward him, staring down into his face, his eyes intense. "Another thing... Don't call me that or alpha bull outside of our quarters. I'll allow you to call me that in private or even in front of Vin but that's where my generosity ends. If you do, I'll give you a spanking you will not enjoy, I promise you that."

Luca's lips twitched, and he lowered his voice. "But you haven't given me a spanking that I *have* enjoyed yet."

Kai's eyes softened, and a smile pulled at his mouth. "That might change tonight as long as our swim heals that awful brand. Once I know that's healed, all bets are off."

Luca lowered his voice even more until it was a whisper. "Is that why you insisted on this swim, *my alpha bull?*"

Kai's fingers tightened on Luca's arm and he pulled Luca against him. His alpha dropped his head and took Luca's mouth until he couldn't help but melt against the taller male.

They were standing out on a bluff where anyone could see them, but Luca didn't care. He twisted his head enough to tighten the seal of their lips before dipping his tongue into Kai's mouth, but he was quickly pushed away, both of them breathing a little harder.

"Enough of that." Kai glanced toward the compound. "Otherwise I may rut with you right here out on the bluff in the open."

"You can't resist me, my a—"

Kai quickly pressed a finger to Luca's lips and shook his head. "Don't."

"I was only going to call you 'my alpha,'" Luca teased. "Is that not acceptable, as well?"

"That's fine. Just don't slip."

That kiss had made his cock swell and harden, but his next question made it worse. "Have you ever rutted in seal form?"

Kai tilted his head and studied him. Luca struggled to keep his face neutral since the thought of rutting while they swam in the Great Sea excited him even more than the kiss.

Unfortunately, Vin might get to know him better than the beta ever planned to since he and Kai had to get naked to slip into their seal skins. And it would be difficult for the servant to miss Luca's reaction to his alpha.

"I have not," Kai finally answered, excitement present in his voice, as well. "Have you?"

"I haven't, either."

A wide smile crossed Kai's face. "Then we might have to see if it's possible."

"Oh, it's possible," Luca assured him.

"But not today, Luca. This morning's swim is for us to bond in seal form and for you to heal. Any experimentation will have to wait for another time."

Luca gave him an exaggerated pout.

Kai threw his head back and laughed. "Again, you're insatiable. How did I get to be so lucky?"

"Because you're just as insatiable and the fates knew we'd be a perfect match."

Kai intertwined his fingers with Luca's and tugged him along since Vin was waiting patiently for them at the edge of the bluff.

"That we are."

Luca wasn't sure he heard what he did since the early winter wind was strong and it stole Kai's words as they strode toward

Vin. Then Vin suddenly disappeared and when they approached the edge, Luca realized there were wide steps cut into the bluff that led to an opening. Kai assisted him down the slippery stone stairway and Luca saw they led to an opening for a large cave that went deep into the earth under the bluff.

"Are the royal skins kept here?" he asked in amazement at the size of the cave. Two guards were posted at the opening and torches held in sconces along the stone walls lit the way as they went deeper into the cave. More guards were posted inside.

"Yes, our skins—and now yours—are highly guarded. There are other caves along the bluff that hold the rest of our colony's skins, and they are guarded, as well, but there are triple the guards in this cave."

"Your skins are more valuable." Luca didn't pose it as a question since he was sure that was a fact. He could imagine someone wanting to steal the skins of royalty. It wasn't as if they were more magical than the seal skins of betas or omegas, but they might be worth more on the black market.

"You know they're not, but some may perceive that they are. Even so, no one wants their skin stolen. It's like stealing someone's soul."

And that was very true. "My skin's already here?"

"It is."

Vin stopped in front of a small alcove deep within the cave and swept out his arm with a bow of his head. "Prince Kai."

"Thank you, Vin."

Kai directed Luca into the alcove as Vin stood in front of the opening, his back to them. Luca watched his mate dig into his pocket and take out the key used to unlock the chest that kept Kai's skin. As Kai opened the lid, he turned to show Luca what was inside.

"Vin had locked your skin in with mine. As you see, it's safe here. You know what to do."

Luca nodded and began to shed his clothes while keeping his back to Vin even though the beta wasn't looking. But that wasn't the only reason why he faced the direction he did. He also wanted to watch Kai as he undressed before him.

Within a couple minutes, they both stood naked, staring at each other. And Luca wondered if Kai admired his form as much as Luca admired Kai's. His alpha was impressive in all ways and Luca was even more impressed when Kai pulled out his skin. The color was a beautiful rich silver, unlike Luca's darker gray seal skin. Luca's did not hold the shine that the prince's did.

He could see now why someone might think the prince's skin was more valuable. It would make some human an impressive fur coat. That thought turned Luca's stomach. To have your skin stolen... to be stuck forever in human form... That would be a living hell. It would be like chopping off the wings of a bird. Maybe the bird could survive but not for long. Selkies needed the sea or they would wither and possibly even die without regular access to a body of salt water.

Even banished Selkies were not denied their skins.

Swimming in the Great Sea brought about a sense of freedom and Luca couldn't imagine not being able to experience that ever again. Even though he was born an omega, being a Selkie was special and Luca had never wished for anything different.

Once Kai slipped his seal skin over his shoulders, he helped Luca put on his. Then with a hand to Luca's back, Kai escorted him out of the alcove, with Vin in attendance, all the way back to the front entrance to the cave.

Luca and Kai stood together at the edge of the cliff and looked out at the Great Sea as it called to them. Luca heard the wind over the waves calling their names.

"Do you hear that?" he whispered.

"I do," Kai murmured back.

"Have you ever heard that before?" Luca asked in wonder.

"No. I can't say I have." Kai squeezed his hand. "Are you ready?"

Luca moved to head down the stairs that led to the surf, but Kai stopped him.

"No, we don't walk into the sea, my omega. We leap. We fly. We feel the rush of the wind as we dive into the vast ocean that gives us our freedom and our life."

As impressive as that all sounded, Luca glanced down at the great distance between the edge where they stood and the crashing waves of the surf. "Is it deep enough? We're very high."

"Are you nervous?"

"Yes?" Luca squeaked.

Kai chuckled. "Don't be. I've done this a thousand times and will do it a thousand more. It's quite safe as long as you're wearing your skin."

"How old were you when you first dove from this cave?"

"A baby. And I didn't dive. I was tossed."

Luca's gaze shot up to Kai as his alpha stared in thought out over the water. "What?"

Kai glanced down at him. "I was tossed. It was my first foray into the Great Sea and our pups will be introduced to it in the same way."

Luca made a strangled noise. "You want to throw our pups off a cliff?"

"Since you see me standing before you, you should realize it's safe."

"It's sink or swim?"

Kai clicked his tongue. "You know Selkies can't drown unless our skins are stolen or destroyed."

"But still..."

"You worry needlessly, my omega. You, our pups... I would never knowingly put you in any danger."

Luca glanced over the edge again and swallowed hard. "I've never had to jump from this great of a height."

"We'll do it together. Once we're in the water, stick close to me. We don't see them often in this area, but occasionally there are Orcas and sharks. And take it from me, you're very tasty, my love."

Luca jerked at his endearment. Suddenly his eyes stung with tears and his words became thick with emotion, "My alpha, did you just—"

Before he could finish his question, Kai grabbed his hand and yanked Luca off the edge. As they free-fell, Luca's stomach rose into his throat.

"Head first," Kai yelled and flipped his body mid-air into a graceful dive. Luca did the same just in time to hit the water. As he dove deep into the surf, his body became one with the seal skin and he surfaced a few yards out from the bluff. They needed to get out of the rough, breaking water, so they could take a relaxed swim. Kai's head broke the water's plane not far from him and he looked in Luca's direction with large dark eyes.

They wouldn't be able to speak to each other again until they were back in human form, but they could very well communicate in other ways.

Closing his nostrils and ears, he ducked beneath the water and, with a kick of his hind flippers, swam toward Kai. Being fluid once again made him giddy with joy. He loved being in seal form. Most Selkies did. To miss out on this because of having one's skin stolen or destroyed would be devastating.

Luca popped up in the water next to Kai. They touched noses and when Kai nuzzled his scent gland, Luca did the same to him. Then they were off, away from the breakers farther out into the Great Sea, swimming side by side, their bodies long and lean as they brushed and bumped against one another.

Kai wasn't kidding when he said he wanted Luca to stick

close to him. Kai didn't let him get more than a foot away from him at any time. If Luca went in a different direction, Kai was there, bumping him with his snout in the direction Kai wanted him to take.

But the long swim felt glorious. The chilly water soothed his skin, and the swim stretched out their sore, tight muscles after all the rutting they had done during the night. After a while, Kai caught a fish to share. Then he captured a squid, Luca's favorite treat to eat while in seal form. Luca ate half and then playfully tossed it back to Kai who caught it and swallowed the remainder in one bite.

Kai chortled and slapped the surface of the water with his fore flipper, splashing Luca, then bumped him forcefully with his snout. Luca circled his alpha, getting closer and closer with each turn until he was rubbing against his mate, twisting and wiggling, encouraging Kai to rut with him out in the surprisingly calm winter sea.

Kai shook his head and growled a low warning. Then, with a sharp twist, swam away, his hind flippers kicking furiously.

Luca reluctantly followed his mate with disappointment. Maybe he could convince Kai to try it during their next swim. The only thing they couldn't do in seal form was knot since it was too dangerous to be tied together out in open water where predators could lurk. But Luca still wanted to experience it. His desperate urge to rut with Kai was nothing like he expected, and he wasn't even in oestrus yet. He could not get enough of his alpha bull.

He had heard that his urges could increase right after coming off the heat suppressants and he figured that was why he was so desperate to rut, as well as to knot. But he'd also been told those impulses should level out. Whether that was true or not, remained to be seen.

They were about two miles out from the shore and the cave,

so it took them a while to swim back even at the steady pace Kai kept. However, Kai was no longer playful during their return, nor did he stick as close as he had when they swam out to the open sea.

Luca knew exactly what had displeased Kai, but it was too late to take his actions back. He should have known his uncontrollable desires might be too much for his new alpha.

He certainly didn't want his prince to wonder if Luca was a Selkie slut, especially after admitting to rutting and knotting with an alpha he shouldn't have. He didn't want to give his new alpha any excuse to send him away.

After a few more minutes, they reached the breakers and Kai helped him out of the rough surf onto the steep stone stairway that took them back up to the guarded cave. Luca didn't even give the guards a second glance as he rushed back to the alcove where their skins would be kept.

As soon as they entered the small nook cut out of the rock, Kai spun on him, his face an angry mask, his voice tight. "I promise, Omega, that we will mate at least once in the sea in seal form. However, after I expressly told you it would not be today, you pushed me anyway. Just like you pushed me this morning to knot you. I let that go. This I will not. I'm your alpha and you must remember your place. If you cannot understand just what your place is, I'll have to teach it to you and, I swear to the great sea gods, it will not be a pleasant experience. Do you understand me, Omega?"

Luca dipped his head, his heart thudding in his chest. "I understand, Alpha. I beg your forgiveness for my disobedience. I'll accept any punishment you feel the need to give me." Luca raised his eyes to meet his alpha's turquoise blue ones. "However, I need to tell you that I find you hard to resist and that's why I keep pushing you. But, again, I apologize for misbehaving and forgetting my place."

Kai's nostrils flared as he stood stiffly but said nothing.

"Prince Kai," Vin called, out of breath as he rushed into the alcove.

"Where have you been?" Kai snapped.

Vin's eyes widened for a split moment at the unexpected anger, then his surprise was quickly veiled. Luca made a mental note to apologize to Vin later when it was just the two of them. Kai's anger was his fault, not Vin's.

"I beg your pardon, Prince Kai. I was called back to the castle and returned here as soon as I retrieved the message I was to give you."

"Which is?"

"King Solomon is demanding an audience with you in the royal library."

Kai's whole body went solid. "Secure our skins, help Luca dry off and get dressed, then escort him back to our quarters. I'll go directly from here to meet my sire."

"Sir, the king wants your omega in attendance, as well."

Luca felt the breath rush from his lungs as he shrugged out of his heavy seal skin and Vin took it from him. Within seconds, Vin was back with a large, fluffy towel, wrapping it around him. Then the beta rushed to relieve Kai of his skin and retrieve a towel for the alpha, as well.

"This can't be good," Kai muttered.

"I'm also thinking this, Prince Kai," Vin said.

"You heard nothing on what it's about?"

Vin shook his head. "That's why I was late in returning to attend to you. I asked around in the servant's quarters whether any information had been overheard, but I found out nothing. I'm sorry, sir."

"You tried, and I thank you for that."

Vin bowed his head and scurried to retrieve their dry clothes.

"When does my father want this *audience*?"

Vin actually stuttered when he said, "Ten minutes ago."

"Shit," Kai barked.

Luca thought a much stronger word would be more appropriate about now. Shit barely covered what they might be walking into when they arrived at the royal library for an audience with the king.

CHAPTER SIX

"On your knees, Omega!"

Kai's father's booming voice shook the air in the library. Kai's jaw tightened, and his lips flattened at the king's lofty command.

As Luca sank to his knees, Kai caught his elbow and jerked him back up. "No, Father, you will not subject my fated mate to that. I'm his alpha, not you."

King Solomon's head jerked back at Kai's defiance. "I am the king. I outrank your being *his alpha*. You forget your place, *Prince* Kai."

This conversation sounded familiar. He had only been reminding Luca of his place not twenty minutes before. He frowned.

"I haven't forgotten anything, Father. But you will not subject my omega, the future *pater* of my pups, to any more subjugation. Now that he's my bonded mate, he's an equal and will not be treated like a lowly servant."

The king's bushy eyebrows rose. "Equal? He's an omega, he'll never be an equal no matter how many times you rut with him, no matter how many heirs he whelps. Any alpha pups he produces will also be above him. Do you understand me?"

Kai gritted his teeth. *Holy Poseidon*, this conversation was like déjà vu. Had he sounded like such a pompous ass when he said similar words in a similar tone to Luca? His eyes slid to his mate who stood next to him, his eyes downcast, his shoulders curved forward slightly.

His omega was not weak-willed and had a fire in his belly, something Kai found very appealing. To see Luca like this in front of his father annoyed Kai to no end.

"Do not let him intimidate you," Kai murmured just loud enough for Luca to hear. Luca didn't even blink in reaction to Kai's words.

Shit.

And to make matters worse, Douglass flitted into the room to stand beside the king who sat behind his gaudy desk.

"You need to leave us. This is a private conversation," Kai said to Douglass, who ignored him and continued to stand just at Solomon's elbow.

"You will stay, Douglass. My son forgets himself. He mistakenly thinks he will take the throne soon."

"I couldn't care less about taking the throne," Kai reminded the king.

"Which is a problem in itself. You are next in line. You should act like it."

"Give it to Rian. He'd be a better king than I. Just because I'm first born doesn't mean that I'd make a good king."

King Solomon's face became ruddy and his jowls jiggled as he shook his head. "It's not only that you were first born, Kai. You are the only heir from my fated mate. That means more than just being the firstborn."

"So, are you saying that your other sons don't mean as much to you?"

The king's spine straightened, and his narrowed eyes pinned Kai in place. But stranger yet, Douglass suddenly stopped flitting and frowned in Kai's direction. Like the little pest should care that the king treated his sons like they were just a bother.

His father's assistant overstepped his boundaries time and time again. He didn't understand why King Solomon tolerated it. Maybe it was because the weasel kissed his father's ass and none of his own sons did.

Kai sighed. "Can we get to the reason why you summoned us? If it's about the Bonding Ceremony... Branding needs to be outlawed. It's cruel, unnecessary and not civilized at all."

"It has a purpose."

"And what is it? Besides claiming a living being as property?"

"It's a reminder to other alpha's that the omega belongs to royalty and isn't to be touched. That's why they are branded and that's why they are so marked in that particular location. When an omega goes into heat, he presents his buttocks to the alpha. Any alpha that sees that brand and continues to rut with the omega will be punished by either being banished or put to death." The king continued with his little pleasant and completely unnecessary lesson. "As a prince you wouldn't want to raise a pup from another alpha, would you? And how long would it take for you to realize that pup wasn't yours if your omega decided to have a secret dalliance?"

"If that occurred, the omega would be punished, as well. We all know that, including Luca."

"That's correct, my son, but how long would the farce go on before it's discovered?"

His father had a point, but Kai still didn't agree with it. "Was my *pater* branded?"

"He was."

"Was your *pater* branded?" Kai asked his father.

"He was."

"There has to be a less barbaric way of marking a royal omega mate if the law calls for it. A tattoo maybe."

"One shift into a seal during a swim and the ink could be pushed out of the skin due to the rapid healing," helpful little Dougie added.

Kai stared at the weasel. "Has it been tried?"

"It has. With Caol's *pater*."

"And it didn't work?" *Bloody hell*, he hated asking anything of his father's assistant.

"It did not. After the first bonding swim, the mark was barely visible."

"It would be too much to actually trust a bonded mate to be faithful, now wouldn't it?" Kai murmured.

"The branding is not why I summoned you and Loukas here," King Solomon stated. "But it does have to do with last night and everything that happened or did not happen during the ceremony."

"There's nothing to discuss, Father. I wasn't going to subject Luca to any more embarrassment than he was already put through. I wasn't going to rut in front of you, my brothers, the guards, and those appointed by the Royal Council. As you like to tell me over and over, I *am* a prince and I do have some power to say no."

His father's expression got hard. "You didn't with this. And it's not the rutting part that we need to discuss."

"Then what part do we need to beat to death?"

"The examination."

Kai froze and so did Luca. Out of the corner of his eye, Kai saw Luca tilt his head and look up at him with wide sea green eyes. Fear, that's what he saw in them. And that blatant fear twisted Kai's guts.

He took two deep breaths to bolster himself then asked, "What about it?"

"Your fated mate came to you not a virgin, and that's disconcerting."

Kai's heart thumped in his chest and he clasped his hands together to hide the sudden tremor.

"Omegas don't have to remain a virgin, Father. That's not a law."

"You are correct, it's not a law under the Royal Council, but this is my colony and I am king here. Your alpha pup will be in line for the throne and I want that pup to come from an omega who has not been defiled."

Defiled. What a nasty word. Kai's frown deepened. "Father, if it doesn't concern me that Luca wasn't a virgin, it shouldn't you. It won't make my pups impure. If it bothered me, I could have rejected him last night. I didn't. I'm fine with the knowledge that he came to me as an experienced omega."

The king continued as if Kai hadn't even spoken. "Not only was Loukas not a virgin, but you didn't finish the bonding ceremony. Which gives me good reason to send him away."

The blood rushed into Kai's ears. But before he could protest, his father spoke again. He was on a royal roll.

"You can find another, a more suitable omega. One that has not been sullied."

He might as well have called Luca a Selkie slut.

Kai needed to do damage control. And fast. "Father, the ceremony *was* completed, but in private. I'm sure you can tell Luca has been *thoroughly* marked. And not just with your atrocious brand. Not only did we bond during our rutting last night, we also swam together this morning in the Great Sea."

His father could not send Luca away now. He couldn't. He shot a quick glance to his omega. Luca looked pale and was shaking like a leaf.

Kai did his best to keep his tone level and under control. Any signs of weakness and his father would try to roll him over.

"Father, just smell him. Check his scent. Our scents are now mingled."

"You know my nose is not like it used to be."

"Then get Marlin or even Adrian."

The king snapped his fingers. "Douglass, call one of the alpha guards into the room."

The little weasel scurried out of the library only to return within seconds with one of the few alphas in the Royal Guard. The majority were betas, but alphas were needed to lead and for an alpha to become a guard, the male had to be already bonded with a fated mate.

The alpha guard bowed from his waist in front of his father's desk. "Your Royal Highness."

Kai rolled his eyes.

"Guard, do you recognize Prince Kai's scent?"

"I do, sir."

"Sniff that omega and tell me if they are bonded."

Kai's body went solid as the guard did as he was told and approached Luca. When he bent down and pressed his nose to Luca's scent gland, Kai's lip curled, and he released a low growl.

Luca stiffened, and Kai chest bumped the alpha guard away from his mate. "Back off."

The guard dipped his head in submission and turned to face the king. "As you see, Your Royal Highness, the prince is extremely protective of the omega. Not only his behavior but their mingled scent confirms it."

King Solomon waved his hand half-heartedly in the air, dismissing the guard. After a quick bow, the alpha strode from the library.

"Satisfied, Father?" Kai asked, reaching for Luca's hand and intertwining their fingers. Luca still trembled, and that made Kai's temper boil.

"Bonded or not, I can still send Loukas away."

"There's no good reason for it." Though if his father found out Luca lost his virginity to another alpha, Kai could imagine that he'd have no say in the king casting Luca aside. Like it or not.

He would have to make sure Luca never mentioned it to anyone. That affair needed to remain a secret.

"I'll give him six months."

Kai cocked an eyebrow at his father while he waited for an explanation.

The king waved a hand at Douglass. "Mark this down. Loukas has six months from this date to become pregnant. If he is not, he will be cast aside, and you will find another. Do you hear me, Prince Kai?"

Six months.

Luca's fingers twitched in his.

Six months was doable. His mate just needed to go into oestrus soon. It was rare that a Selkie in oestrus did not become pregnant, and knotting was the reason why. It ensured that the alpha's seed was planted deep and remained planted long enough to take root. The only time an omega struggled to get pregnant during a heat cycle was if the omega had some sort of medical issue.

Or the alpha did.

Infertile alphas weren't unheard of. But if Luca didn't become pregnant because of Kai's deficiency, the king couldn't blame Luca for that and send him away. Could he?

Bloody hell, his father was capable of anything when he had a hair up his ass.

"Mark it in your little planner there, Dougie, that Luca will be carrying my heir way before the six months are up."

"May I suggest you give a sperm sample to the doctor to make sure you're capable of siring pups, *Your Highness?*"

Kai pursed his lips as he studied the pain-in-the-ass beta who was always much braver when he hid behind the king. "You won't always be standing behind my father, Douglass," he reminded his father's personal assistant.

King Solomon slammed his hand on the desk, making Luca jump next to him. "Enough! Just do your duty, Kai. And now that Douglass has mentioned it, maybe you *should* be examined by my doctor and supply a sample for testing."

"My swimmers are fine. Quite healthy and abundant. I'll get my mate knocked up as soon as he goes into heat."

Solomon sighed and said with a wearied tone, "Whatever you say. Just get it done. Now, leave us."

Thank the sea gods, they were being dismissed. Kai turned on his heel and strode toward the door, Luca hurrying to catch up or have his arm pulled from his shoulder.

"One more thing," King Solomon called out.

Kai cursed and stopped dead, not bothering to turn to face his father.

"There will be one more condition. The first pup he whelps better be an alpha. If it isn't, both Loukas and your firstborn will be banished."

Kai closed his eyes, struggled to regain his breath, then pulled Luca out of the door, slamming it behind them.

As Kai escorted Luca down the corridor toward their wing, he kept his voice low when he said, "You need to go into heat soon."

"It's not like I have control of it. Rutting with my fated mate should bring it on. And we've been rutting."

That they have. But it was only the second day. Not that it normally took long for an omega to be coaxed into oestrus. Technically it could happen right after the Bonding Ceremony.

"I don't want to be sent away, my alpha," Luca whispered.

Kai lifted their entwined hands and pressed a kiss to the back of Luca's. "I don't want that, either. But heed this, you must never mention that affair with that other alpha. Do you hear me, Luca?

It's very important. My father will have you banished or even put to death if he finds out. Look how he's acting just on the fact alone that you're not a virgin. If he found out it was an alpha and that you were knotted..."

Kai had a lump in his throat just at the thought of the power his father held in his hands. Especially when it came to Kai's fated mate.

"I'll forget it ever happened," Luca assured him.

"Good. It's for the best. Now..." Kai stopped abruptly in the hallway and looked around to make sure it was empty, and no one was close by. He pushed his omega back gently until he was pressed to the stone wall.

He dug his fingers into his mate's dark blond hair and tilted his head back. He could see Luca's pulse thumping wildly in his neck. "I need you to listen to me, Luca. How my father treated you is unacceptable in my eyes. Do you understand I don't feel the same way he does?" Kai would never want to turn into his father, who could be cold and callous, even when it came to his own sons.

Luca winced as he tried to nod his head since Kai had a fistful of his hair. But he did not want Luca avoiding his gaze.

"I'm sorry about how I spoke to you earlier in the cave. I was unfair."

"No, you were right. I was disobedient." Luca smirked as he said, "I deserved that tongue lashing."

Kai fought back his smile. He was glad to see his behavior, as well as his father's, had not dampened Luca's spirit. "Interesting choice of words. But still, I apologize, and I hope to do better in the future."

Kai lowered his head and brushed his lips lightly across his omega's. He didn't want to do much more than that since he needed to remember that they were still out in the corridor. And anyone, including his brothers, could come along at any moment.

"Do you plan on making it up to me?" Luca asked, his green eyes sparkling like the sun reflecting off the sea.

A smile tugged at Kai's lips. "How would you like me to do that?"

"In countless ways."

Kai released a feigned weary sigh and rolled his eyes. "That sounds tiring."

Luca chuckled. "Yes, that's the plan."

"I need to save up energy for when you go into oestrus. That will be a trying time."

"Hmm. I can't wait."

Kai arched a brow at him. "You might think differently once you go into heat. I've heard that during some longer cycles, the mating couple need betas to come in and feed them, so they don't perish from starvation and exhaustion."

"How embarrassing," Luca murmured.

"Believe me, you might be so out of your mind that you won't mind a full blown human parade with high school bands passing by while we rut."

"Maybe I should go back on heat suppressants," Luca murmured.

"You cannot. You heard what my sire said. You must be pregnant within the next six months or he will banish you... Or worse."

"Then let's get back to the subject of you making up for your rudeness to me."

"When do you want me to begin?" Kai brushed a thumb across Luca's bottom lip. He was tempted to nibble on it.

Luca touched Kai's thumb with the tip of his tongue, then gave him a naughty smile. "Right now," he said, his voice husky.

"We have dinner."

"Dinner can wait."

Kai sighed. "I'll have Vin prepare something that can be reheated later."

Luca ran a hand down Kai's chest, making his nipples bead into points. "That sounds like a plan."

He stopped his omega's hand from dipping into the waistband of his pants and jerked him away from the wall instead. He smacked Luca on the ass to get him moving back to their quarters. "Now, let's go try to jump start your oestrus."

———

Luca's fingers dug into Kai's scalp as his alpha bull's mouth sucked on the swollen crown of his cock. He tossed his head back and cried out as Kai licked down Luca's length, then scraped his teeth along the skin on his way back up. Then his alpha did it again. Kai's tongue left a wet trail down to his sac and his teeth made Luca gasp on the return trip to the top.

Not only did precum bead on the head of his impossibly hard cock, but slick was trickling down his crease at an alarming rate. His prince needed to take him soon, but he also wanted to come down his alpha's throat. Though, Luca wasn't sure if Kai would allow that. If he wouldn't, then Kai needed to quit sucking him because it wasn't going to take much more to make him come. His balls were already pulled up high and tight.

Luca gasped when Kai shoved two fingers into his slick hole and found his prostate.

"My prince... I... uh... I'm..."

Kai didn't stop, his mouth continued to suck, his fingers continued to massage that sweet spot, and Luca's hips popped off the mattress as he orgasmed uncontrollably, both his cock and anus throbbing intensely as he spilled deep within Kai's mouth.

His chest heaved as he tried to catch his breath. A few moments later, Kai released him and slipped his fingers free.

Luca opened his eyes, not even realizing he had squeezed them shut when he came. With a tilt of his head, he peered down his body at his alpha, whose head was still between his thighs.

He liked the sight of that. Kai's turquoise blue eyes were hooded and though Luca couldn't see it, he was sure his alpha bull was raring to go. Luca began to roll onto his belly to offer Kai his ass.

His prince stopped him. "No. Your brand is healed now. It doesn't hurt, right?"

"No." Luca's heart fluttered at the thought of them finally rutting on his back, face to face.

"Then stay where you are. I want to mount you like this."

His anus squeezed in excitement, then loosened in anticipation, preparing to take his alpha bull's generous cock.

Kai shifted until the head of his erection pressed against Luca's hole and Luca held his breath, waiting for him to push forward.

"Keep your knees to your chest, Omega. And give me your mouth." With that, Kai thrusted forward at the same time he captured Luca's lips in a kiss so deep it stole his breath.

Luca groaned as his alpha bull filled him and managed to stretch him even as loose as he had become. The amount of slick he was producing made the entry painless even with Kai's size.

He reached down and grabbed Kai's ass encouraging him to thrust harder and faster. And he complied, not breaking the kiss. His prince's tongue touched his and then tangled, his fingers digging into Luca's hair, holding him still so he could take the kiss even deeper.

Finally, Kai broke away and shoved his face against Luca's neck, licking along the pounding lifeline along his throat.

"You smell so good, my omega. I've marked you as mine and that's the best scent in the world. The perfect aphrodisiac."

Luca agreed. He loved being claimed as Kai's. He loved that

Kai's scent was now mingled with his, that it identified him as the prince's fated mate.

But he was both worried about coming into heat and excited about carrying his prince's pup. Every time they rutted, he became more bonded to Kai, more closely connected.

Luca wrapped his legs around Kai's back and tilted his hips in an attempt to take Kai deeper. He cried out when his alpha nipped at his nipples, first one then the other. He worked his way back up biting and licking until he reached Luca's mouth once more.

"Do you like when I bite you, Omega?"

His alpha's growled question sent a shiver through Luca. "Y-yes."

"Do you like when I fuck you?"

"I do."

"Do you like when I fill you with my seed?"

"Yes, my bull, I love when you fill me up and mark me as yours."

"Are you ready for my knot? Because you aren't begging for it yet."

Luca lost his breath. He couldn't answer. However, he didn't have to. His response was his canal squeezing Kai's cock and his alpha grunted, his body stuttering, his rhythm breaking.

"That's it, my omega. Squeeze me tight."

Kai curled over him and scraped his teeth over one of Luca's now sensitive nipples, causing his back to arch and for him to cry out.

"That's it, Luca. Let me hear you. Tell me what you want."

"I want you, my bull. All of you. Please..."

"Please what?"

Luca's eyes rolled back as he begged breathlessly, "Please... oh, please..."

"Luca, tell me."

"I..."

"I know what you want and I'm going to give it to you. But not until you tell me."

"Please, my bull... my alpha... my mate, give me your knot. I need your knot."

Kai slammed into him hard and ground deep, his cock swelling. Then it happened. His knot expanded, and Luca's ring tightened around it until they locked together. Kai grunted, his cum spurting deep inside Luca, his hips still flexing slightly as he did so.

Finally, he stilled, and Luca dropped his legs to the mattress as Kai collapsed on top of him, breathing hard. Luca wrapped his arms around him as his prince tucked his face against Luca's neck once more.

"There can't be anything better in the world right now than being tied to you," his alpha murmured against Luca's throat.

The only thing Luca could think that would be better was if he was carrying his alpha's pup right now so there was no risk of the two of them being separated.

He only met his fated mate yesterday, and it already felt like they'd been a bonded couple forever. He didn't think he could live without his prince. Not now. Not ever.

He might even be in love with him.

To be banished or even just cast aside so Kai could take another...

Luca rubbed at the tightness in his chest.

He hoped he went into oestrus soon. Otherwise, that love, that bond, could very well be destroyed.

CHAPTER SEVEN

KAI STIFLED a yawn as he opened the bedroom door and directed Luca to go ahead of him. They were both freshly showered, and he was starving. Vin said he'd leave something in the oven to keep warm. What it was he had no idea, he only hoped it hadn't dried up into something petrified. They had spent a little more time in bed than what Kai expected.

It took at least ten minutes for them to separate and then even after that he had a difficult time pulling away from his fated mate, so they had spent a while actually snuggling.

Him. Prince Kai of the North. *Snuggling*.

He snorted and followed Luca out to the kitchen. When his omega stopped short in the entranceway, Kai slammed into him with a grunt.

"Luca!" he exclaimed in surprise.

"I am sorry, my alpha," Luca said quietly, stepping aside.

Kai moved around him and then froze.

His four brothers sat around the dining room table, grinning at them. Hell, Caol even winked.

He prayed to the almighty Poseidon to give him patience.

"You two are very noisy," Marlin announced.

"Let me tell you," Zale began, his blue eyes sparkling, "listening to you two rut like beasts makes me look forward to finding my own fated mate."

"Not me," Caol replied to Zale and Marlin with a smirk. "I can make a beta cry out and moan like that. You two must be doing it wrong. I don't need to be bonded to anyone any time soon."

"That's because you're a Selkie slut, Caol. You can't keep it in your pants," Rian said dryly.

"Yes, unlike you, Rian, I enjoy rutting," Caol said to his older brother.

Rian opened his mouth to argue but Kai cut him off.

"Yes, we know, Caol, and you do it often," Kai said as he moved farther into the room.

Caol shrugged. "It's good practice."

Rian snorted and crossed his arms over his chest, pinning his gaze on Luca. "Cat got your tongue?"

Kai looked over his shoulder to see Luca still standing frozen in the doorway, his beautiful green eyes downcast in submission. "Luca, they might be princes, but they're all assholes. Please feel free to treat them as such."

"We are not nearly as bad as Father," Caol said.

That certainly was true.

"Well, at least four of us," Marlin stated. "Rian is. He wants to be crowned King Asshole."

And that was true, too.

"He's already achieved that, I think," Zale muttered.

"Keep it up, brothers, and you will see me act like a king asshole," Rian drawled.

"Oh, we haven't seen the worst of you yet?" Caol asked, his eyebrows high on his forehead.

"Very funny."

"Okay, why are you all here?" Kai asked with a sigh as he walked back to Luca, put a finger under his chin and lifted his face. He gave his mate a smile and then a quick kiss to his forehead before pulling him along with him over to the table.

"Tonight was your night to host dinner," Rian announced.

"Hmm. Vin didn't remind me of that. He knew we... Never mind." He pulled out a chair and indicated with a wave of his hand that Luca should sit. He did.

"It's nice to see you for once with your clothes on, Loukas," Zale said.

"Luca," Kai corrected.

"What?" Zale asked, confused.

"He answers to Luca," Kai repeated.

"Ah, yes. Our sire has been calling him Loukas, so it was stuck in my head. Luca. Bringer of light!"

"Let me call Vin to come serve us." Kai hadn't planned on disturbing his beta servant tonight, but now with his brothers expecting a meal...

"It's late. He's probably in his bed by now. My servant is standing outside the door," Rian stated.

"Of course he is," Kai said under his breath.

Rian pushed from his chair and disappeared, moments later returning with his beta servant, Ford, on his heels. "Did Vin already have something prepared?"

Kai glanced toward the oven and he sniffed. "You can't smell it?"

"I smell sex and lots of it," Rian answered.

"We did shower," Kai murmured.

"Your whole wing reeks of it. Wait until Luca goes into heat," Caol said. "The whole compound will smell like a human whore house."

"Why doesn't it surprise me that you know what one smells like?" Rian asked their youngest brother.

Caol shrugged and shot him a smile.

Rian clapped his hands and said, "Ford, serve us whatever Vin prepared. And hurry, because it's late and I'm starving."

Marlin frowned at his older brother. "He's standing right there, why not just ask him? No need to clap to get his attention."

"Because clapping makes the asshole feel important," Zale stated.

"Listen, you handle your servants however you'd like and let me handle mine however I'd like."

"And this is why Vin thanks me daily for being assigned to me and not you, Rian. I treat him with respect. You should try it sometime."

Rian waved a hand around in the air, reminding Kai of how similar to their father Rian was. He was definitely a chip off the old Selkie block.

"Ford doesn't mind."

Kai glanced over at the servant in question as the male pulled something out of the oven. The beta wore a poker face.

"I can help him," came quietly from the end of the table where Luca sat. He pushed to his feet.

All five of King Solomon's sons commanded, "Sit," at the same time and Luca plunked back down in his chair.

"Ford can handle serving us dinner, Luca," Kai said a little more gently. "He's fine."

"And now you're the fated mate of a prince, you don't do chores like a beta," Rian reminded him.

Color flooded Luca's cheeks. His omega needed to get more comfortable around his brothers, if not his father. Kai didn't like how he got mousy around any of them. There was no need for it.

Within minutes, Ford had steaming plates set out in front of them. Kai finally settled into a chair next to Luca. He leaned over the hot food and inhaled. Seafood casserole. Kai's favorite.

"I swear," Caol said with his mouth full already, "I'm going to steal Vin away from you. Beck doesn't ever make me this and if he did, it wouldn't be this good."

"Beck is a shitty cook, Caol," Zale said. "You only keep him around to rut with him when you can't find anyone else."

"I have needs and Beck doesn't mind. In fact, he encourages it."

"Needs!" Zale shouted and slammed his hand on the table, laughing. "The pup has needs."

Caol frowned. "First of all, I haven't been a pup in a long time, Zale. And second, yes, I have needs. Everything needs to remain in good working order."

Kai turned to Luca who was eating quietly. "My youngest brother is what the humans call a man ho."

Luca choked on his mouthful of food and Kai laughed as he patted him on the back.

As soon as Luca got his food swallowed down and had sipped at the glass of wine set in front of him, Kai addressed all his brothers. "Did any of you pay attention during the Bonding Ceremony lesson?"

Marlin put down his fork and frowned. "No, but I certainly paid attention last night."

"I wish I would have because if I knew what it involved, I would have feigned sick last night and skipped it," Zale added, not even pausing while shoveling the delicious casserole into his mouth.

"I paid attention," Rian said, patting his lips with his napkin.

"Of course you did," Caol shouted.

Rian's brows furrowed. "Caol, we're at the dinner table, don't shout."

"Yes, *Father*."

"So, I assume you all are against the practice of branding our mates? Did you all find it as horrific as I did?"

"The smell..." Caol groaned, then pushed his half-eaten plate away.

"Oh Poseidon! Did you have to remind us of that?" Marlin said then covered his mouth and turned slightly green. His eyes slid to Luca. "Luca, I'm sorry for you not only being subjected to that last night but for us bringing it back up again tonight. Kind of like my dinner."

Kai reached a hand under the table and squeezed Luca's knee before sliding a palm up his thigh. One of Luca's hands dropped below the table and covered Kai's. Kai turned it palm up, and they intertwined their fingers.

"What are you doing under the table?" Caol asked, his eyes narrowed, his lips curled slightly.

"Nothing. Just holding my mate's hand. Nothing more," Kai answered innocently.

Caol made a noise. "Uh huh."

"Ah, you have gone soft, brother," Zale said with a knowing smile. "But I'm happy for you."

Kai tipped his head. "Thank you. I'm very pleased with my match. But back to the subject at hand... We need to do away with this branding. Hell, the Bonding Ceremony all together."

"A bonding ceremony is necessary, Kai," Rian reminded him.

"Yes, but not on a platform in front of everyone. Even Father!" Marlin exclaimed.

"And that weasel Douglass," Kai muttered.

"Him, too," Marlin agreed with a nod.

"Right, it can be done in private like the common folk do. And they have no need to *brand* their mates!" Kai squeezed Luca's hand.

"We are royalty, brother. We can't just do away with traditions. That would make us no better than those common folk. You did exactly what they do. You went to your room to rut."

"After poor Luca was branded and inspected like a steer

before a livestock auction," Marlin said. "If that's what my future mate has to look forward to, then I want to pass on all of it."

Rian sniffed. "We are all obligated to produce heirs. It's the law."

Caol shrugged lazily. "So have me arrested. I can produce an heir. It just might not be a legal heir in the eyes of the Royal Council."

"A bastard," Rian spat.

"If you say so, Rian," Caol, said. "Maybe you need to take the royal scepter out of your royal ass."

Marlin laughed. "Now you're asking for the impossible. Just like asking Father to put aside these ancient so-called traditions that are barbaric. They're completely unnecessary."

"Agreed," Kai said. "So, will you all back me if we approach Father about changing the way the Bonding Ceremony is held? And the branding?"

"He's not going to simply agree to do away with it. You know how stubborn he is. Plus, there's the Royal Council..."

"But if you all refuse to participate in the future ones..." Kai directed a pointed look at King Solomon's second oldest son who sat across the table from him. "You are next in line, Rian. You would need to put your foot down. Take a stand."

"Bah! Rian go against traditions? He's Father's clone," Zale said.

"Rian?" Kai prodded.

Rian tilted his head as he considered what Kai said, then he lifted the wine that Ford had fetched him. "Let me think about it."

"What's there to think about? You seriously don't mind your fated mate being scarred for life with our insignia?" Kai asked.

"There's a reason for it," Rian answered with a shrug.

Kai grumbled, "That's exactly what the king said."

"Of course," Zale muttered.

"Can we get off this dreadful subject and onto something more interesting?" Marlin asked. "Like Luca. Tell us about your family, Omega."

Shit.

The fact that he never bothered to ask Luca about his family smacked Kai upside the head like a two-by-four.

Luca slipped his fingers from Kai's as he sat back in his chair.

"Only if you want to, Luca. Don't feel pressured."

"Holy Neptune, Kai, nobody is pressuring Luca to do anything. We just want to get to know him better," Marlin exclaimed.

"You're just being nosey and that's why you all showed up for dinner. You knew we'd be busy..." Kai sighed, deciding it was better not to finish that sentence. "You could have easily had dinner elsewhere."

Zale swatted a hand in Kai's direction. "Get over yourself, Kai. We truly want to get to know the newest member of the family."

Out of the corner of his eye, Kai noticed his mate relax slightly in his chair. Maybe this would be good for Luca. He did need to get to know Kai's brothers as they *were* now family. And Luca needed to feel comfortable enough around them to approach them with anything he needed. Especially if Kai wasn't around for some reason. Though, for the most part, he expected Luca to be by his side while Kai did his royal duties. The only time he might not be able to do that would be if his omega was heavy with his pup.

He studied his mate sitting at the end of the table and pictured him with his belly swollen, carrying Kai's firstborn son. A warmth stirred through Kai at the thought. He never cared before if he produced heirs, but now... Now he couldn't wait. It made him want to drag Luca from the table and back up to his bed, his brothers be damned.

"Yes, Luca, tell us about your family. Any other siblings? Are both your father and *pater* alive?" Zale encouraged.

"Yes, my—"

"He speaks!" Caol crowed, interrupting Luca.

"Caol, quit it," Zale admonished him. He turned his attention back to Kai's mate. "Go on."

"My father and *pater* are both alive and still very much in love. I don't have any siblings. After I was whelped, my father didn't want to put my *pater* at risk by having another pup, so..."

Luca's eyes slid to Kai, who gave him a slight nod in return, encouraging him to continue.

"So, they did what they needed to do to prevent getting pregnant again."

"That's illegal by Selkie law," Rian stated, sitting stiffly in his chair.

"It happens all the time, Rian. Yes, in the scrolls there's a law about preventing pregnancy but it's common knowledge that it's done all the time. They produced one pup, which is perfectly acceptable. And would satisfy the Royal Council. Especially when that one pup turned out to be a royal's fated mate," Kai clarified.

Rian sat back in his chair with a frown. "What colony are you from? I'm not sure if Douglass mentioned that."

"Cascadia."

Rian lifted his brows. "The Pacific Northwest. So, you're used to the cold climate we have here in the Northeast."

"Yes. I prefer it."

"Have you been to other colonies?"

"Yes—"

"He was presented several times, Rian," Kai interrupted.

Rian's eyebrows shot up once more. "Oh? To who?"

"Who is not important. He's my fated mate, and that's all that matters."

"I imagine you'll miss your parents being so far away?" Zale asked gently.

"Yes... I..." Luca shot Kai a questioning look. "I hope I'll be permitted to visit them or have them come visit me here."

"Of course, Kai's not a monster. He would never stop you from spending time with your family. Especially after you bear pups."

"Thank you for answering for me, Marlin," Kai said, his voice heavy with sarcasm. "But he's right, Luca. You wouldn't be able to travel alone, but we could always plan a visit or have them come here. They'll be our pups' grandparents, after all. And I'm sure much more loving than our own sire."

"You can say that again," Zale muttered. "It wouldn't take much to be more loving."

"So, what do you do, Luca?" Rian asked.

"Do?"

"Yes, your occupation. You did work in your colony, correct? I can't imagine you sat around hoping to become a kept omega."

"Rian," Kai said low in a warning tone.

Rian looked across the table at him. "What? It's a valid question."

"It's the kept part that I don't appreciate," Kai clarified.

Rian lifted his hand. "Fine. I'm sorry, Luca."

Kai twisted his head to look at his mate. A bead of sweat appeared. Kai frowned. Were all the questions Rian shooting his way making him nervous?

Luca drew a hand across his forehead, whisking it away.

"Are you okay?"

Luca glanced at him, a bit flushed. "Yes. It's okay. I..." He turned his attention back to Rian. "I was a teacher."

"A teacher! That's wonderful!" Rian crowed. "We could always use more teachers in our colony. Such a loss for yours, though. Did you enjoy it?"

"I loved it."

Another bead of sweat popped out and rolled down Luca's forehead.

"Luca," Kai breathed as his chest got tight and his stomach knotted. Something was wrong with his omega.

It had to be more than nerves.

"Are these questions making you uncomfortable?" Kai asked.

"They are simple questions," Rian began in protest.

"No, I don't mind them."

"What ages did you teach?" Rian continued, ignoring Kai's glare.

"All ages, but I love the six to eight range the best. They are so open to learning at that age."

Rian nodded with a smile.

Suddenly, Luca's breathing sounded labored and a fine sheen of sweat covered his whole face.

"Luca, are you all right?" Kai asked, now getting deeply concerned. It was not overly warm in the room. In fact, Kai liked to keep his quarters on the cool side.

"I... I... I'm sorry. I suddenly..." Luca picked up a napkin and patted at his face.

Zale sniffed the air. "I don't think he's all right, brother."

Marlin's nostrils flared, too, as he picked up the strong scent that rose up from Luca. "No, I agree with Zale."

Kai glanced around the table to see his brothers' eyes pinned on Luca like a pack of wolves staring at a tasty rabbit. *Bloody hell.*

"I think your mate's coming into heat, Kai," Caol stated, shifting in his seat, his fingers digging into the table.

"No one moves," Kai announced, pushing to his feet, trying not to snarl at his siblings. "Stay seated." He looked toward Luca, who sat with wide eyes as he stared worriedly at the sudden change of attitude in the princes. "Luca. Get up slowly. Move slowly and go up to our bedroom and lock the door. Do not open it until I knock and announce myself. Do you hear me?"

Luca nodded and jumped to his feet.

"Slowly," Kai reminded him, struggling to keep himself together. The scent was getting stronger and his mind was beginning to spin. His own body began to overheat, and a raging hard-on pushed painfully against his zipper. He glanced at his brothers.

Rian had his eyes squeezed shut, his breathing rapid, and he had the arms of his chair in a death grip. Zale had his face turned away from Luca, his jaw tight. Marlin's chair was pushed slightly away from the table, so Kai couldn't miss the erection he sported since his pants were tented sharply. And Caol...

Caol had eyes only for Luca, his face flushed, as well. "Kai..." his youngest brother groaned.

"Go now!" Kai barked at Luca.

Luca moved too quickly, drawing the attention of all of them, but Kai kept an eye on his brothers as he heard his mate rush up the steps to their sleeping quarters.

He didn't breathe until he heard the door slam.

His alpha brothers needed to leave, and they needed to do it immediately. His instinct was to fight them all, and he tried to beat that back. There was no way he could take on all four of them. He needed to remind himself that they all needed to remain civil and attacking his brothers was not acceptable. They didn't want to breed with Kai's fated mate, but the scent could tempt them to do just that. That distinct smell could draw them to an omega going into oestrus.

"We need to go," Rian stated between gritted teeth.

"Yes," Kai struggled to get out, his fingers curling into tight fists. "Now... please... before..."

With a stiff nod, Marlin bolted to his feet. "Let's go. Now, brothers. We need to leave them."

"Someone please inform Vin about what's happening," Kai said as he watched his brothers force themselves toward the door.

"Do you want us to tell Father?" Caol asked.

"No, just Vin. Make sure the weasel doesn't find out, either. Last thing I need is him sending in someone from the Royal Council to observe. Now go. Quickly, please."

After his brothers filed out, along with Ford, Kai remained in place between the entrance to his wing and the stairway to their sleeping quarters just in case one of his brothers decided to challenge him for Luca.

They wouldn't mean to, but they might not be able to help it. For good reason, none of them had ever been around an omega in oestrus before. At least, he didn't think so, though he wouldn't put it past Caol. So he wasn't sure how any of them would act. But brothers or not, he would protect his fated mate from being bred by another alpha no matter what. Even if it meant killing the other alpha.

And doing so would certainly cause a major family rift.

After a few moments, Kai blew out a breath, swiped the sweat off his brow and headed upstairs, forcing himself not to run.

When he reached the top of the steps, he immediately moved to the bedroom door and tried it, finding it unlocked.

Luca did not lock the door as instructed. He had disobeyed. *Again.*

When he pushed the door open, the sight and smell that hit him made him lose his mind.

CHAPTER EIGHT

Luca couldn't stop plunging his own fingers into his slick, loose hole. It was leaking uncontrollably and throbbing with need. With his face down on the bed, he held his ass in the air in preparation for his alpha to take him.

And he needed that done immediately. He thought if Kai would just rut with him this suffering would lessen. That somehow the desperate need to be filled with his alpha bull's seed would calm the craziness.

"Please... please... my alpha bull... hurry," Luca called out when he heard the door open.

A chill ran through Luca even though his body was covered in sweat. He did not like this out-of-control feeling at all. This was nothing like the first time he'd gone into heat when he was younger. This was so much more intense.

Most likely because he was now at a prime breeding age.

"My alpha, please..." He couldn't help sounding whiny. Because he was. His head was spinning rampant and fucking himself with his own fingers was not helping. His erection was so painful that he was trying to jerk himself off to relieve that discomfort, too. But it wasn't working. His own hand was not enough on either end.

"Please, my bull!" he cried out once more into the pillow.

"I'm coming, Luca. I'm almost undressed."

His alpha's deep voice so close by made a shudder run through him. "Hurry! I need your knot now."

"Okay, I'm... *bloody hell.*"

Luca heard buttons landing on the stone floor and bouncing across the room.

Within seconds, the bed sank behind him and his mate was there, sliding his engorged cock along Luca's slick crease.

"Move your hand, Luca, let me in."

With a whimper, Luca slipped his fingers from his own hole and then Kai's cock was there in their place.

"You're so open," his alpha groaned.

There was no time for foreplay. "I need you."

Then with one thrust, his prince was taking him hard and fast. This rut was about getting the job done, not exploring each other, not getting to know each other. No, this was all about getting to the end as quickly as possible.

Luca tilted his hips as he continued to fist his own cock, hoping for relief. The head was so sensitive that he jerked violently every time he touched it.

"You're burning up, my omega."

"Hurry, knot me." Luca's canal squeezed Kai's cock tightly, encouraging the alpha to pop his knot. "Please, I need your seed. I need you to put your baby inside me so this ends."

Kai didn't answer. All Luca heard over the roaring in his ears was his alpha's ragged breath and his grunts. Their skin was now slick with sweat as Kai pounded into him hard enough to jolt Luca's body with each thrust.

"Please, please, my bull, give me your knot!" he cried out once more.

"It's coming, Luca."

"Now!" he begged.

"It's coming," Kai assured him, his voice catching.

When Luca felt his alpha's cock swell impossibly larger, his eyes rolled back in his head. "Give it to me, Alpha."

Kai groaned and then grunted as his bulbus glandis expanded larger than it had when Luca wasn't in heat. His teeth sank into the back of Luca's neck, pinning him in place on the bed.

Luca cried out at the slight pain from both the knot and the bite, but he still couldn't get enough of Kai. He ground back against him and squeezed his sphincter tight until his prince came so hard that his whole body jerked violently. Kai's cock twitched deep inside Luca as the cum spurted fiercely from him. Luca's womb opened to accept everything his alpha gave him, and Luca gasped at the odd feeling. He'd never experienced it before since he'd never rutted while in heat, but he had been told what would happen.

Kai continued to shudder against him until he was finally empty. Then his alpha's hand was pushing his away from his cock, and took up the stroking rhythm along Luca's erection, squeezing the head on every upstroke until Luca quivered beneath him and cum shot out of him so intensely that it landed on the sheets almost as far as Luca's head.

Luca closed his eyes reveling in the feeling that his alpha's seed now coated his insides. And with luck, one seed would be strong enough to take root. He knew his heat cycle would subside as soon as it did. If not, they could be doing this frantic rutting for a while, he just didn't know for how long. Even if this mating didn't take, his cycle would only last so long until his body would go into a reset mode to rest and then a month or so later he'd go back through it again. Wash, rinse, repeat. Until he carried his alpha's heir.

"I was rough," Kai said gruffly into his ear after he'd released

Luca's flesh from his hold. His alpha's breathing had slowed somewhat but his heart still thumped furiously against Luca's back.

"No. I'm fine. It's all good. I don't mind it rough."

"I know. But these ruttings aren't for pleasure."

While that was true... "It doesn't mean we can't enjoy them."

"You say that now, but I have a feeling neither one of us will enjoy it after a while if my seed doesn't take in one of these first few times. I was losing my mind."

"So was I. I was afraid it wouldn't be you coming through the door. In my state, I would have accepted any alpha. At the time, that didn't scare me, but now the thought that could've happened does."

A long silence preceded Kai's next words. "I told you to lock the door."

"I'm sorry. I was distracted." Luca paused. "And desperate, like I said. I would have accepted any alpha."

"I know. This is why you must never travel without me. You understand that, right, Luca?"

"Yes. Unless I go back on heat suppressants... Not now," he added hurriedly. "I mean later after I whelp your heir."

"We shall see."

"I have a feeling the way we responded is only going to get worse as the cycle goes along, my prince. This is only the beginning of my heat."

"Then let us hope my seed does its job sooner than later."

"Yes, let's hope," Luca agreed.

"If during your heat, the knot is our only slice of sanity, let's also hope that the knotting lasts as long as possible."

"Can we get me off my knees as of now, my alpha? I have a feeling I will be on them a lot in the next day or so."

Kai chuckled, and with care, guided them onto their side and into a spooned position. "Is that better?"

"Yes, my prince, much better."

"Please, Luca, call me Kai in our quarters, especially when we are being intimate."

Luca twisted his head to look over his shoulder at his alpha. "I like calling you my prince or my alpha bull."

"I know. But why?"

"It turns me on," Luca confessed.

"Because you see me as more dominant?"

"Yes, very. I like that you have the power to dominate me."

"I don't want you to feel submissive to me. You will be the *pater* to our pups. You are my mate."

"Am I an equal? To a prince?"

"Yes, in my eyes you are. Others?" Luca could feel Kai shrug behind him. "Maybe not in everyone's eyes. But no matter what, in our quarters always feel that you are equal and can speak freely. Even to my brothers. You are not to submit to them in any way. As my fated mate you hold some power. Understood?"

"Understood. How about outside of our quarters? Should I submit to them then?"

"I will have a talk with them. If any of them treat you without respect, you come to me immediately. And do not let Douglass run over you, either. He's a bossy little b—" Kai made a noise, then finished with, "beta."

Luca smirked. What little he'd seen of the king's smug assistant had proven that fact.

"Next time we rut, can we do it face to face? I'd rather see you when we talk."

"We can do that, but I have a feeling as soon as our tie releases you'll be presenting your ass in the air once again. It's not something you may be able to control," Kai murmured into Luca's neck.

Luca reached back and cupped his prince's head, holding

him close. He loved when Kai pressed his nose to his scent gland. It made butterflies flutter deep in Luca's belly.

He was definitely falling in love with his alpha. Which was a good thing since they would be mated for the rest of their lives. He was extremely happy with the choice the fates made.

"I'm glad it was you," Luca said softly.

Kai lifted his head slightly. "Come again?"

"I'm glad it was you," he repeated.

"Through the door first? Me, too. It could've gotten ugly if it wasn't."

"Well, that, too." Luca shook his head. "But that's not what I meant."

"What did you mean, my omega?" Kai asked, stroking Luca's sweat-dampened hair.

"That the fates chose you for me."

Kai brushed his lips along Luca's shoulder and then pressed his mouth to Luca's ear. "I'm just as glad. You please me greatly, Luca. Please don't let anyone dampen your spirit, including me. If I'm harsh with you, please, please, take me to task. I don't ever want to make you unhappy."

Tears stung Luca's eyes at his alpha's touching words and he reached for Kai's hand that laid along Luca's hip. Kai met him halfway, intertwining their fingers and squeezing.

"While we can still think clearly, let me ask this: Do you *want* me to dominate you when we rut?"

A shudder skittered through Luca at Kai's question. "I like it, my prince. I think it's part of my omega nature to want my alpha to take control."

"Hmm, I see. You purposely want to be naughty, so I give you a good *tongue-lashing?*"

Luca smiled. "Yes, I enjoy your *tongue-lashings.* It prepares me for your huge cock."

"Ah, so you've noticed my enormous member?" Kai teased.

"It's hard not to when it's shoved up my ass."

Kai moved his hips slightly and Luca gasped at the pull of the knot. It shot a bolt of lightning down into his cock, making it stir.

"Your oestrus made me swell more than ever tonight."

"I noticed, my well-hung bull."

Kai raised their clasped hands and pressed a kiss to Luca's knuckles. "Was it painful? I apologize if it was."

"Just slightly at first. I quickly got used to it."

"Mmm. Good. I came so hard I thought I saw stars. If I come that hard every time during your cycle, I may very well pass out before this is over... *Shit*."

Luca turned his head. "What?"

"My knot..."

Suddenly, Kai slipped from him and, immediately, Luca began to sweat and shake. His body's instant reaction was crazy.

"I..." Luca started but his thoughts swirled away. Unable to control himself, he rolled to his belly and lifted his hips back in the air. "My prince," he begged.

"Luca, I haven't recovered yet..."

Luca glanced behind him and saw Kai's cock still swollen impossibly large and dripping with both slick and cum. "But..." He panted. "I need you."

"Luca," Kai groaned.

"Take me, my bull. I need you to take me. I'm not pregnant, give me your pup... please."

"Luca," Kai barked, grabbing his cock and stroking it. "On your back!"

Luca shuddered at his forceful command.

"Now, Omega! Present yourself to me on your back!"

"I... can't." He was powerless to lower his hips. It was like they were frozen in place.

With a twist, Kai had lifted Luca up and shoved him down onto the bed on his back.

"You do what I say, Omega. No excuses. Do you hear me?"

"Yes!"

"Present your hole to me. Pull your knees back and show me. Let me see how slick and open it is. How it's begging for my cock."

Luca was now drenched with sweat once again, his body shaking uncontrollably. It wasn't just his oestrus causing it, it was his alpha's commands. His eyes rolled back with the ecstasy of it all.

Luca pulled his legs back and, with both hands, spread his ass cheeks. "Take me, my bull."

"I will take you when I'm ready, Omega, not because you beg me. I'm in control here."

"Y-yes, my bull." Luca wanted to cry, beg and scream for his alpha to hurry. His body was burning up with need and there was only one way to stop it.

"Do you want my cock, Omega?"

"Y-yes."

"Now?"

"Yes... *please.*"

"I should make you suck it clean first."

Luca groaned. While normally he'd want that, the need to relieve his suffering was too great. He would not enjoy being forced to lick his alpha's cock clean at that very moment. There was something else he wanted more.

With relief, Kai thrust forward, taking him roughly. Luca whimpered as his alpha bull's sac slammed against his ass over and over as he pounded into him furiously, Kai's own sweat dripping onto Luca's belly.

With gritted teeth, Kai demanded, "Did your other alpha take you this hard?"

"No... my alpha."

Kai slammed his hips against him once more. "Did you enjoy his cock inside you just as much?"

"No!"

"Is this my hole now, Omega?"

"Yes, my alpha, it's all yours."

"Will you ever let any other alpha inside you?"

Luca gasped because with each question, Kai slammed him as hard as possible. "No. Only you."

"Will you take another alpha's seed?"

"No. Please give me yours."

"Do you want me to fill you up? Do you want my cum to cool your heat?"

"Yes! Please!"

"Do you want my pup inside you?"

"I do. Please give me your pup."

"I want to see your belly swollen with my pup."

"Yes. I want that... Please, please, my bull..."

"Please what, Omega?"

"I—"

"You what, Omega? What do you want?"

"Your knot. Your seed. *You*."

Kai's words softened. "You have me, my love. I'm yours."

Luca's head spun, and he cried out as Kai knotted him once again, his alpha's ass clenching beneath Luca's fingers which dug into his flesh. His alpha twitched as he came once more. Though not as intensely this time since it was so soon after their last knot.

Kai's breath rushed in and out of him rapidly as he pushed as deep as he could into Luca. Luca's sphincter muscle tightened once more, tying them tightly together. He rolled his head back on the pillow as Kai's seed spilled inside him, bringing a soothing relief once again.

His racing heart slowed slightly, and after a moment, he tilted his head enough to observe his prince curled over him, his body still heaving from the effort and the orgasm, his face shoved into Luca's neck.

Luca dragged his fingers up the damp skin of Kai's back, then wrapped his arms around his prince's neck. "I love you," he whispered.

Kai stiffened. After a moment the prince lifted his head and Luca stared up into his Caribbean blue eyes which had become dark like a stormy sea. "Luca," he said softly.

"I'm sorry if you feel that it's too soon."

"My bringer of light, it's not that's it's too soon. We are fated mates for a reason. Love will come naturally because of our strong connection. But don't confuse your oestrus for love."

He wasn't. But maybe admitting it only two days after being presented to his alpha had been foolish. "Again, I'm sorry, my prince." Luca dropped his gaze from Kai's.

Kai grabbed his chin and lifted it back up. "Look at me. I have very strong feelings for you, too. You're my bonded mate. You never have to apologize for something you think you feel."

Luca wasn't just thinking it; he was sure he *knew*. He never felt any sort of emotion when he rutted with the alpha who took his virginity. While their rutting had been enjoyable and satisfying, that was all it was.

Even though this was only their second night together, Luca still felt that deep connection Kai had mentioned. It was unmistakable. Yes, maybe his hormones were raging due to oestrus. But still...

He couldn't describe how he was feeling as anything other than love. And Kai himself had called Luca "my love" a couple times, so he figured his prince felt the same way. And also with what Kai said right before knotting...

Luca must have been wrong.

"Luca, we are tied together face to face. I thought you wanted that so we could talk more easily during our *down time*."

"I did. I do."

"So, what do you want to discuss?"

Nothing really, he just wanted to stare into his alpha's handsome face and look into his beautiful blue eyes as they knotted. He wracked his brain to come up with something.

He asked the first thing that crossed his mind. "Will I be able to teach here in your colony?"

Kai's head jerked back. He was probably not expecting that question to be asked so soon. "It would be out of the ordinary for a royal's omega to work. We have betas as instructors in our colony's school. Your job would be raising our pups. Would that not be enough for you?"

Though it should be, as it was an important job, Luca also loved to teach. Even though he became a teacher knowing he might have to give it up once he was bonded, he had hoped his fated mate would allow it and he'd be able to continue with his passion.

Before Luca could answer, Kai continued, "We've just been bonded. Why don't we wait until after you've had our first pup and then we can see if you're still interested? To be honest, even if you are, the king might not allow it. I'm just warning you now. And anyway, with you being off heat suppressants, we'll have to see how often you go into heat after your first pregnancy. You wouldn't be able to teach during oestrus. Otherwise, the students might get a lesson they might not need to learn so soon."

Luca smiled. "True. Unless I'm teaching Sex Education 101."

Kai chuckled. "I'm assuming you're not a Sex Ed teacher."

"No, since that's a human class. Our school had health classes geared toward our race, of course. The teacher covered bonding, rutting and oestrus, things that would affect us Selkies."

"I'd assume they did not cover that atrocious royal Bonding Ceremony."

"No, unfortunately, since most omegas would not be presented to royalty. The alpha heirs of our king were privately taught."

"As was I. And my brothers." Kai pressed a light kiss to Luca's mouth but pulled away before Luca could encourage him to take it deeper. "That's something to think about, Luca. Teaching our own sons as well as my brothers'. My father might not frown on it as much if you only taught the royal heirs."

"That's an idea." And better than nothing. "As long as I'm not putting a beta out of a job."

"It has been a long time since we've needed a beta tutor. The last one appointed was very old and died shortly after Caol became of age. There's been no need to replace him. It'll be a few years before our pups are old enough to need one, as well."

"But if the king would allow it, I would love to do it."

Kai brushed the hair away from Luca's face and stared down at him without saying anything for longer than normal. Luca fought the urge to squirm under his direct gaze.

"Is something wrong?" Luca asked finally.

Kai smiled softly. "No, I was just picturing you standing at the front of a classroom instructing our pups as well as my future nephews."

Luca gave him an answering smile. "I could, too. And they will be *our* future nephews." He suddenly lost his smile. "I would just need to survive the whelp."

Kai swallowed so hard, Luca could see his Adam's apple bob. "Don't even say that."

"Would you miss me, my prince, if I didn't?"

"Luca!" Kai said sharply. "That isn't even funny."

He wasn't trying to be funny. He was being very serious. "But a lot of omegas don't survive—"

"Besides a midwife, the royal doctor will be present, and I'll have a human doctor present, as well, if needed. Nothing will happen to you, I—"

"You what, my prince? Do you promise? I know you can't do that. Omegas dying during whelp is all too common for us Selkies."

"Enough of this talk. It's morbid." Kai shifted suddenly, and the knot pulled at Luca's anus, making him cry out in pain. "I'm sorry. I didn't mean to move that much, Luca. Just don't... please don't talk about leaving me."

It probably was a sensitive subject since Kai's own *pater* died while whelping him. How sad to have never known the male who brought you into the world. Luca was lucky that his survived and he couldn't imagine his life without both of his parents.

"I'm sorry you never knew your *pater*," Luca said softly.

"You apologize way too much, my omega. But I am, too. I was lucky I had such a great nanny."

"A human, is that correct?"

"Yes. I would like you to meet her. I still love her dearly."

"As much as a stickler as your father seems to be about tradition, I'm surprised he used a human female. It's unheard of and I thought frowned upon by Royal Council standards."

"Normally it would be. However, we had no lactating omegas in the colony at the time of my whelp and I would have died if he had waited for one to travel from another colony. Meesha lived in the town nearby and had just lost her own infant to SIDS, so she was thrilled to mother me. It was an emergency situation that turned out for the best for both of us. We bonded immediately and still remain close."

"Did she wet-nurse any of your other brothers?"

"No. The king made sure that a nursing omega was available nearby during the whelping of my brothers. And it was a good thing, too. Though Rian and Marlin didn't need it since both their *paters* died during a later whelp, Zale and Caol did. And... *ah...*"

Luca raised his brows at the expression that crossed Kai's face. "What?"

Kai grimaced. "Get ready, my omega, we're going to be untied again in a few seconds."

Again, Kai's cock slipped from him, this time leaving a messy trail of fluids in its path.

"Oh no," Luca groaned, unable to stop himself from flipping back onto his belly as the shakes and the sweats started once more. "My prince..." he begged.

"Holy Poseidon, I swear your heat will be the death of us both and we won't even have to worry about the whelp," Kai muttered as he dug his fingers into Luca's hips and pulled them up and back. Then he began to thrust uncontrollably into Luca once more.

CHAPTER NINE

"How does anyone survive this torture?" Luca cried as he presented his ass for what seemed like the millionth time in two days.

Two days.

Two *long* days. Kai swore his cock was going to fall off. His head spun and not from the heady scent of Luca's oestrus. No, from dizziness caused by exhaustion and dehydration.

He wasn't kidding when he said that Luca's heat cycle might kill them both. His stomach was empty and twisted. He and Luca both had lost weight to the point where he was starting to see his mate's ribs.

This madness needed to stop and the only way it would was if his seed took root in Luca's womb or the heat cycle ran its course.

The only time they had any relief was during knotting and, even then, that relief was short lived. As soon as the swelling went down, the urge to rut became intense once more. They had no time to shower. No time to change the sheets, which were now stiff from caked-on dried sweat, slick and cum. No time to grab food or even water.

He now wished Luca had brought heat suppressants with him to end this.

But then, if Luca didn't become pregnant soon, his father would send him away. At the least. And that couldn't happen either.

Kai wouldn't lose his mate. Not after he just found him.

Or the Seekers did, anyway.

Even so, he prayed to Poseidon that this would all come to an end soon. The worst part was because he was so exhausted it was taking him longer and longer to knot Luca and he hardly had the energy to even thrust anymore. His body was on auto pilot, doing what it needed to do to make sure his bloodline continued into the next generation.

"My prince," Luca cried, a tear rolling down his cheek. He had to be as sore and tender as Kai was from all the rutting. Why wouldn't he get pregnant?

Was Luca infertile?

Was Kai?

If either was true, then they were doing all of this for nothing. Kai was getting frustrated and annoyed since this was not enjoyable for either one of them. Even during the knots, they no longer had the energy or desire to even carry on a conversation. They would lie quietly and try to recover just the slightest bit.

Kai couldn't imagine that he even had any sperm left in his body. He was probably shooting puffs of dust.

If Luca didn't get pregnant this cycle, they'd have to do this all over again in a month or so. Kai groaned.

They were so dehydrated that they had even both stopped sweating. Kai ground his back molars as he couldn't control the thrusting motion of his hips. He needed to pop his knot, so he

THE SELKIE PRINCE'S FATED MATE   115

could take a break. But he was worried he didn't have the energy to do simply that.

Without warning the bedroom door flew open and Kai turned his head with a snarl.

Caol stood in the doorway, eyes wide, face pale as he observed the scene before him. "Holy sea... men!"

"Get out!" Kai growled with everything he could muster. If Caol fought him right now to rut with Luca, he wouldn't be able to win that fight. Caol could take Luca and even might be able to impregnate him before Kai could. His lip curled at his alpha brother.

Caol jerked a half step forward, but his body appeared unnaturally stiff as if he fought with himself to keep from approaching the bed. "Vin's worried. Hell, we all are. It's been two days."

His youngest brother wasn't telling him anything he didn't already know. Kai shouted, "Get out!" once again.

Caol shuffled a little closer, his hands fisted tightly against his thighs. "You two need to eat..."

"Out, Alpha! This is my omega and I will not let you take him."

"Kai... I don't want him..." He took another step deeper into the room. "Shit..."

Kai couldn't stop thrusting into Luca even though his brother stood watching. "I will kill you if you come any closer," Kai snarled, baring his teeth.

Caol shook his head as if to clear it and then backpedaled quickly. "I'll send Vin in."

The door slammed shut and, thank the glorious sea gods, Kai's knot finally swelled enough to tie Luca to him. His mate whimpered in relief and Kai almost did, too.

"This is madness; it can't go on."

"What can we do?" Luca asked, sobbing into the already drenched pillow.

Kai struggled to slow his breathing before answering his mate. "I don't know besides you getting pregnant or hoping your cycle doesn't last much longer. I never expected it to be this bad."

He helped move the two of them onto their sides and he swept Luca's matted and soaked hair away from his face. "I'm sorry, my love, that you have to suffer so."

"You are, too."

Kai opened his mouth to answer him, but the door opened once more and Kai's words turned into another low growl of warning.

"Kai... Sir. You and Luca must eat. You have to hydrate."

Vin was so very right.

"May I approach the bed, sir?"

"You may," Kai answered weakly, relieved that Vin had arrived to assist them. The beta didn't make Kai feel possessive, like he needed to protect what was his... which was Luca. "You'll have quite a task cleaning up, Vin, after this is all over. I'll apologize right now. And I'm also sorry you are seeing us in this state."

Vin handed him a large bottle of water as well as Luca. The caps had already been removed, and they were all quiet while he and Luca guzzled down the much-needed fluids.

But it still didn't feel as though it was enough. Not nearly enough.

They needed to take a swim in the Great Sea after all of this. That may rejuvenate their worn bodies.

"I brought sardines and kelp as well, sir."

Kai sniffed the air, but he could detect nothing over the smell of sex and the addictive scent of Luca's heat cycle.

"Leave it on the nightstand."

"No, sir, I need to make sure you both get at least some of it into your bellies. I will feed you if necessary."

It was embarrassing enough that he and Luca were tied

together naked on the bed covered in dried fluids, but now his beta wanted to feed them by hand? "Vin..."

"Sir, I'm not leaving until you at least eat something. And until you finish that whole bottle of water. I have more to leave behind, as well."

Kai sighed. "Fine. Feed Luca first."

"But—"

"Luca first," Kai said firmly, then closed his eyes to rest while Vin attended to Luca.

"Do you know how long this might last?" Kai heard Luca ask Vin.

Kai wasn't sure what Vin knew about heat cycles since betas were infertile. They could not impregnate an omega, nor did they go into oestrus because, like alphas, they had no womb.

"Two or three days typically... Five at the most."

Someone must have instructed Vin in Selkie breeding. Which, now that Kai thought about it, made sense. The beta servants to royalty should know all about that stuff since they were tasked with assisting their alpha. Which in turn meant assisting their alpha's omega. Which could mean assisting with rutting and oestrus which Vin was doing right now.

Though, if Vin had known anything about the royal Bonding Ceremony, he should have warned Kai.

"Five?" The panic was clear in Luca's question.

"Have you ever been in heat before?" Vin asked gently.

"I began heat suppressants after my first one. But I was young, so it was short and mild. My parents ended up locking me in my room to keep me safe until it was over. Then, afterward, they immediately took me to the doctor and put me on suppressants."

"Well, hopefully you'll get pregnant by my alpha prince soon. I can't wait to have babies around. I've been looking forward to them for some time. The last baby in the castle was Prince Caol. And that's been some time ago."

"Is it because you can't have any yourself?"

"One reason, yes. I wish..." Vin paused. "Let me go get some warm washcloths to at least wipe your faces. Is that acceptable, sir?"

Without opening his eyes, Kai answered, "Do what you need to do, but quickly. I'm not sure how long I'll be able to hold this knot."

Kai listened as Vin rushed away. He must have drifted off because the next thing he knew, Vin was wiping his face with a wet cloth. Kai wanted to protest, but he didn't have enough energy to even open his eyes. Instead, a sigh escaped him.

"There. Somewhat better. Sir, open your mouth, you need to eat at least half of this bowl."

Kai did what he was told as if he was a newborn pup himself. The sardines tasted salty and delicious, but the kelp... Well, it was kelp and not his favorite. However, it was packed with a lot of dense nutrition which Luca and he both needed.

"I will make kelp and sardine smoothies and bring them in for your next round."

Luca groaned at Vin's words. Kai wanted to, as well. Neither of them was looking forward to their next round. Hell, he wasn't sure he'd want to rut with Luca for a long time after this. He had certainly had his fill.

Never in his life had Kai thought he could turn down sex. But right now... the thought of rutting again...

He needed to somehow make his knots last longer. It could be simply mind over matter. Maybe he could will himself to remain tied to his mate.

Kai moaned miserably. Who was he kidding? His mind was like a bowl of mushy oatmeal.

"Can you bring fruit smoothies instead?" Kai asked, still unable to open his eyes.

"No, I'm told kelp and sardines are the best fuel to eat during heat."

"How about if I give you an order to bring a banana and strawberry smoothie instead? Maybe add some peaches?"

"Then I would disobey, sir. I'm only doing what's best for you and the future *pater* to your pups."

Kai didn't miss Vin's voice getting excited at the prospect of having a baby around. He knew Meesha would be just as thrilled.

Hell, Meesha didn't even know Kai had found his fated mate.

"Vin, get a message to Meesha and let her know about Luca."

"Don't you want to tell her yourself?"

"Who knows if I'll survive this."

"She'll be so happy to have a grandpup to cuddle," Vin continued, ignoring Kai's macabre answer.

"We have to get Luca pregnant first."

"No," Vin said. "*You* have to get him pregnant. I can't do that; I can only go make you smoothies to get you through the next couple of days."

"Oh no, don't say a couple of days," Luca moaned. "This needs to end soon."

"Then your prince needs to get the job done."

Kai forced his eyes open just so he could glare at his beta servant. "Does it look like I've been slacking?"

"Maybe just your little royal swimmers are," Vin said as he gathered the empty water bottles and bowls.

"Seriously, you forget yourself, Vin."

Vin smiled and headed toward the door. "I'll go make those smoothies. I may even throw in a dash of seaweed and squid."

"Sounds delicious," Kai called out. "Can't wait. Make sure to include one of those little umbrellas in our glass."

"I'll do that." Then the door slammed shut.

Kai blew out a breath.

"I like him," Luca said quietly.

"That's good because we're stuck with him."

"He cares about you."

"And he will fall in love with you, too."

"I hope so. I've left everyone I know behind."

His poor omega. Ripped from his family and sent to the other side of the country to live with strangers and be forced to rut with one, too. "You'll make new friends here soon enough. This colony is relatively large. And the humans' town isn't so far away. They're quite friendly and we share many resources."

"Are the humans here like the ones in Cascadia?"

Kai twisted his head to study Luca's profile. "How do you mean?"

"I know females still exist in the human race but are they the only ones that can bear their young?"

"No. There are a few males in town that are hybrids. They were born to male omega shifters, but their sires were human males. There aren't a lot of them, but they do exist."

"Can you as an alpha get a human female pregnant?"

"I think so, yes. But I have no desire to rut with a female. Human or otherwise."

"Can these hybrids shift?"

"Can the hybrids in Cascadia shift?" Kai asked in turn.

"Only a select few."

"Then I'm sure it's the same here. The human genetic makeup can't be that different on the west coast than the east coast. Especially since humans move around all the time."

"True." Luca paused, then leaned his head back against Kai's collarbone with a sigh. "The water and the food helped. I feel a little better now."

"I'm still whipped," Kai admitted, brushing a knuckle along the hollow of Luca's cheek. After this was over, he'd have Vin make plenty of food to fatten up his omega. "And I think my balls have shriveled up into raisins with overuse."

Luca reached back and cupped Kai's sac. "Hmm, yes. Your formerly impressive package is not so impressive right now."

Kai chuckled, which surprised him. He had to be feeling a little better himself. He hadn't laughed in the last two days. "My cock still fills your hole, my omega."

"That it does."

"*Ah, shit.* Not for long though. I am sorry, Luca, but get ready. Is there any other position which will be easier for you?"

Before Luca could answer, Kai's knot released, and he groaned as instinct instantly took over making him pin Luca onto his belly as he took his omega mate once more.

CHAPTER TEN

Luca sat in the back seat of the long, black car, staring out of the rear passenger side tinted window while holding onto Kai's hand as if it was a lifeline.

"There's no reason to be nervous, Luca."

Luca turned to his prince. His turquoise blue eyes were filled with concern, a lock of his dark-as-midnight hair falling across his forehead. He looked so much younger when it did that. "Yes, there is. It's been four months, Kai. Four. And I'm not pregnant yet. Your father has already begun the search for a new mate for you."

"That's not going to happen."

"And you'll go against the king?"

"If I have to."

"Kai... I love you. You know that because I've told you a million times now. But it's not worth being banished for. Or worse!"

Kai squeezed his hand, then lifted their clasped fingers to his lips, brushing a kiss along Luca's knuckles. "My love, you are my fated mate and you will be the *pater* to my heirs. *All of them.*"

"There will be none if we don't figure out why I can't get pregnant."

"If it's my fault, then my father will just have to accept that fact. There would be no reason to cast you aside as I wouldn't be able to produce an heir with *any* omega. Whether you or any other of his choosing."

"He'll still blame me."

Kai sighed. "He's stubborn."

Luca returned to staring out of the side window. In the four months he'd been at the Northern Colony, he hadn't had a chance to explore outside of it. Kai talked about the town of Seaport, where the humans lived, as well as some shifter hybrids, but he hadn't taken him there yet, nor had he met his alpha's former nanny/wet-nurse Meesha.

Maybe today wasn't the best day to meet the human female that had stepped in to "mother" Kai as a pup. Luca was already a bundle of nerves as it was.

"Why the human doctor, my prince, instead of the royal doctor?"

"As I explained prior, I want to hear the truth from someone who doesn't have my father's ear."

Luca's stomach churned, and it wasn't due to being hungry, even though he hadn't eaten a thing at breakfast. Vin had chided him for not eating, telling Luca that he needed to keep his weight and energy up for the next round of oestrus.

His cycle had returned twice more after the initial one and just as intense. And both times it had lasted three days like the first time. *Three incapacitating days.*

The only thing they had to look forward to afterward was going for a long swim together in the Great Sea. Luca cherished that alone time with Kai. Their swims made them feel free but at the same time very connected. And during that time, they could forget about the pressure to create an heir to the throne. They simply enjoyed each other.

The serenity of swimming alongside Kai made the suffering during oestrus almost worth it. But what would make it totally worthwhile would be carrying his alpha's baby.

If his womb was defective...

Luca closed his eyes in an attempt to tamp down his worry. Having the male carry the offspring was not normal in most species and had only developed out of necessity. But that didn't mean there still weren't issues with it. Where the female carrying the young had been done for millions of years, the evolution of omegas being able to conceive was still in its infancy in comparison. So, things were more likely to go wrong.

Every time he had gone into heat, he did feel the entrance to his womb open. So, at least he knew that part of his anatomy was working properly. But what if he wasn't carrying any eggs? What if he was barren?

A tear slipped from beneath his closed eyelids and before he could sweep it away, to hide it from his mate, warm fingers brushed along his cheekbone.

"No need for tears, Luca. We'll go into exile if we need to. I'm not giving you up just so I can produce heirs to the throne. I have four other brothers who can do just that."

"You're the firstborn son, though, my prince. The king keeps—"

"Then if the issue does not lie with me and ends up being you, we can use a surrogate."

Luca's eyes flew open, and he stared in shock at his alpha. He yanked his hand free from Kai's. "A surrogate?"

Kai shrugged. "It's not unheard of."

His voice became higher pitched than he'd like. "But you would need to rut with another omega!"

"Yes, but—"

"I would wither and die inside if I knew you were mating with another."

Kai's brows furrowed. "Don't be so dramatic, Luca. There would only be one purpose for it. It would be nothing but a means to an end."

"Right. And if it turns out to be you, do *I* get to rut with another alpha?"

"Luca," Kai growled.

"I thought so."

"If it is you, we don't need to have pups at all. If I wanted pups with someone other than you or a surrogate, I would be required to cast you aside first. Don't you get that?"

"What a mess," Luca mumbled.

Kai grabbed his hand again and pressed it along his warm, muscular thigh. "It'll be fine, I—"

Luca cut him off. "Don't make promises you can't keep, my alpha."

"Look, let's get through our appointment, then I'll introduce you to Meesha, who's been dying to meet you, and when we get back we'll go for a nice long swim, yes? Just me and you."

"Mmm. Can we try what I want to try?"

Kai cocked an eyebrow. "To rut in the Great Sea?"

A small smile tugged at Luca's lips. "Yes, please."

"But you can't push me to knot you, it's way too dangerous."

Luca's smile widened. "I won't. I—"

"Don't make promises you can't keep, my omega," Kai echoed him.

Luca laughed, some of the tension leaving his body. "We can find a secluded spot."

"Right and have our brains bashed to smithereens from striking our heads against the rocks. It'll be hard to swim to safety with my cock stuck deep up your ass."

Heat swept through Luca. "Maybe we can do it along a sandy beach or a quiet cove somewhere."

"We'd have to swim for miles to find one."

Luca looked toward the front of the vehicle where two royal guards sat in the driver's and passenger's seat on the other side of the tinted privacy divider. "We could have the guards drive us to a safe shoreline somewhere."

"You are so naughty," Kai scolded but his smile did not match his words.

"You love it."

"I do." Kai sighed. "I'll give it some thought, okay?"

Luca squirmed in his seat. "Soon, yes?"

"Yes. I'll think on it soon. And that's one promise I can keep."

Luca wiggled closer to Kai and leaned his head on his shoulder. "Thank you, my prince."

"You're welcome, my love. I will try to give you the world, but it may not always be possible."

"I'm fine as long as I get to stay with you."

Luca heard Kai's sharp intake of breath. "That's the plan."

"And you knock me up," Luca added quickly.

Kai chuckled softly. "That's also the plan." He pressed his lips to the top of Luca's head. "I'm so lucky the Seekers found you, my mate."

"Me, too," Luca breathed.

The car slowed, and Kai looked out of the window. "We're here." He brushed his fingers along Luca's cheek, tucked them under his chin and lifted his face for a kiss. "You may have to help me produce a sample of my seed."

"A little plastic cup doesn't do it for you, my prince?"

"No, only you do it for me, Luca. Nothing or no one else."

Luca pinned his lips together to keep from bawling like a baby at his mate's words. Kai helped him climb out of the car when the guard opened the door. They walked into the clinic, holding hands.

———

"Finally!" the human female who flung open the door screamed, making Luca wince.

Luca only noticed her curly grey hair, rosy cheeks and her sparkling brown eyes before he was smothered against some generous breasts as she clutched him to her, squeezing the breath out of him.

"About time," she scolded Kai, still not letting Luca go.

"Well, we've been a bit busy," Kai answered. "Don't squeeze the stuffing out of him, MeeMee."

Meesha clicked her tongue at Kai but released Luca from her death hold, but not letting him go completely. She shoved him a step back and inspected him up and down. "You're perfect. Such a compliment to my Kai-bear."

Luca snorted. "Kai-bear?"

"Oh, yes, Kai used to be such a cuddle-bear. After I'd finish nursing him, he'd cling to me and scream his head off if I tried to put him back in his crib."

Luca's lips twitched. "And just how long did you nurse him?"

"Meesha," Kai warned in a low voice.

Meesha swatted a hand toward Kai. "Up until he was two. Then the king put his foot down and said no more." Her voice got stern, and she shook her finger like the king would do. "He gave the *order* that I was not to raise a coddled weakling."

"The prince certainly isn't that."

"No, he isn't." Meesha finally let Luca go and she hugged Kai just as tightly, making joyful sounds as she did so. "I've missed you, Kai."

"And I you. You know you can come to the compound at any time. You have free rein to come and go as you please."

The relatively tall but well-rounded female waved a hand around. "I've been busy, too."

Kai lifted a brow. "Doing what?"

"I have book club, knitting club, euchre club... you name it and us retired nannies have it."

"Ah, so you won't have any time for your future grandpups, then?" Kai asked in a teasing tone.

"Oh please, you won't be able to stop me from entering the compound once the first one is born. I will climb the walls if I have to."

"That would be a sight to behold." Kai leaned in the doorway with a smirk. "Can we actually come in? Or is our visit going to be held out here on your stoop?"

Meesha's dark brown eyes twinkled. "You're still not too old for me to put you over my knee and spank you for being a smart-mouth." She stepped back from the doorway, letting them both enter.

Luca glanced around. It was a typical human house. Small and quaint. The perfect size for one or two people to live in. It was clean and organized, but still full of knickknacks. For some reason, humans *loved* knickknacks.

Kai grabbed his elbow and directed him to the right into a room off the foyer. Definitely a living room since it had a fireplace and a couch with what looked like a hand-knitted blanket covering it.

As Kai steered him to the couch, Luca ran his fingers over the blanket. "This is beautiful." The colors were bright and cheery and lit up the small room.

"I'll make you one. Right after I'm done knitting baby blankets for your pups."

Kai groaned under his breath and Luca glanced up at him in question.

"I heard that, Kai. If Luca wants me to knit him a blanket, I'm going to knit him a blanket. You might be a prince and an alpha, but Luca is now my son-in-law, or omega-in-law or whatever, by default."

Luca stifled his giggle.

"Sit! Relax. I'll get us some tea."

As Kai dropped to the couch, Luca remained standing. "May I help?"

"No. Sit down. And if you two want to do some cuddling and smooching on my couch while you wait, I won't complain." She winked at Luca.

"Don't encourage him, MeeMee. Because you might come back out to find us knotted on your furniture. He's insatiable."

Meesha lifted a brow. "Then why aren't you..." She lifted a finger. "Tea. Then we'll talk. I'll be right back."

She scurried from the room and Luca settled next to Kai. "Can we smooch?"

Kai laid his arm over Luca's shoulders and pulled him close. "Are you in the mood after that exam?"

"I'm always in the mood... Well, except after the third rutting during oestrus. By then..."

"Understood."

By the time they'd rutted for the third time in a row during the beginning of his cycle, they were both ready for a break. And they knew none was coming until his cycle ran its course or Luca was impregnated.

"Exam or not, I still want to smooch. I've never *smooched* before."

Kai rolled his eyes. "We *smooch* all the time."

"But it sounds much cuter when she calls it smooching."

"Give me a kiss and shut up," he grumbled, leaning over.

Luca met him halfway, wrapping his hand around the back of Kai's neck, letting his fingers play along his dark hair which seemed to be getting longer in the back. His prince took the kiss deeper than Luca expected he would on the couch of his former nanny and suddenly Luca lost his breath and his heart began to race.

His cock was even starting to stir. And it was not the best time for that. He tried to pull away but Kai cupped his cheeks and held him in place. His tongue swept through Luca's mouth and a groan slipped from Luca's throat.

He pressed a palm to Kai's chest and pushed him away.

Kai sat back, laughing. "You wanted to smooch."

"But now I'm hard."

Kai dropped his gaze to Luca's crotch. "That you are."

"It was bad enough when I had to help you ejaculate into that cup. I was so hard that I was in pain. Then I had to get into that paper gown *with* that hard-on. The doctor kept staring at the wall behind me because I think he was embarrassed."

"He's a doctor, Luca. He's used to natural bodily functions."

"He's lucky I didn't come all over the exam table when he stuck his fingers up my ass."

"Okay, now *that* would have been embarrassing." Kai frowned. "And I don't like the idea of you coming because of someone else sticking something inside you. I'm the only one who should make you come."

Luca shook his head. "If it had happened, it wasn't like I could control it!" He narrowed his gaze on his prince and then gave him a naughty smile. "Maybe you would've had to give me a spanking tonight, though. Hmm. Maybe I should have done it."

"Luca, really. If you want me to spank your ass until it is bright red, just say so. I'll be happy to oblige. I don't need a reason other than you wanting it."

"La la la la! I did not just hear that last part!" Meesha sang as she entered the living room carrying a tray with a tea set.

Heat rose into Luca's cheeks as Kai jumped up, took the tray from her and placed it on the low table in front of the couch. He poured the steaming tea into three delicate china tea cups and passed one each to Meesha and Luca.

"I told you he's insatiable, MeeMee. This is why we've been too busy to visit."

She laughed and sank her weight into a recliner facing the couch, placing her tea cup on a side table. She immediately leaned over, picked up what looked like long metal sticks from a basket and began to move her hands quickly as she created something.

"Are you knitting?" Luca asked, fascinated.

"Yes, would you like me to teach you?"

"No!" Kai shouted. "My mate's not going to be sitting around knitting like an old woman."

"Kai!" Luca exclaimed. "That was rude."

Kai shot him a look.

"Well, I *am* old, but he just doesn't want to be overrun with knitted items. Like a toaster cozy. Or a sweater. Or even boxers."

"The boxers made me chafe," Kai muttered.

"They were only to be worn to bed, not under your pants."

"I don't wear anything to bed," Kai announced.

"He doesn't," Luca seconded.

"I didn't need to know that," Meesha mumbled.

Luca picked up his tea cup and took a careful sip. It was minty but sweet, too. He liked it. "What are you making?"

Meesha's hands stilled, and she looked at him like he was nuts. "A blanket for your firstborn."

"Oh," Luca answered softly, glancing quickly at Kai.

Meesha's gaze landed on Kai, too. "Okay, so spill it. What the hell is going on? Why aren't you pregnant yet?"

"The king said I'm broken and need to be replaced."

Meesha's jaw dropped. "To your face?

"You know my father," Kai said dryly. "He has no tact." He lifted his cup to his lips, drained half of the contents then placed it back on the tray.

"Uh huh. We *all* know how your father is. There were many times I wanted to strangle him."

"You should have," Kai said under his breath.

"Luca, I doubt you are broken. You've only been trying for..."

"Four months," Luca finished for her.

Meesha glanced at Kai. "That's not normal for a Selkie, right?"

"No. If both mates are fertile and healthy, it's not normal."

"Well, you both look healthy. So what did the doctor say?"

"Everything appears normal," Luca stated. Kai shrugged in agreement.

"And your sperm, Kai-bear?"

Kai groaned. "MeeMee, really."

Luca coughed as some of his tea went down the wrong pipe. Kai patted him on the back. "His sperm is quite viable, Meesha," Luca stated when he could finally speak.

And there was plenty of it, too. They only needed a small sample in the cup, the rest had gone down Luca's throat. It had tasted super salty since Vin kept sneaking sardines, kelp and seaweed into their food.

"Even though the doctor said everything looked normal, he also stated that the heat suppressants I was on for so long could have messed up my cycle. Suppressants can make heats longer, more intense and even make it harder to conceive because you're messing with nature."

"I can understand that. But aren't they necessary?"

"Yes, unless an omega wants to find themselves pregnant from a random alpha," Kai answered. "But he also said that it may take a while for Luca's body to become receptive to my... seed."

"The problem is, the king is already hunting down another omega for my prince!" And that thought turned Luca's stomach.

"What? Why would he do that?"

"He only gave us six months for me to get pregnant or I'll be cast aside."

Meesha frowned and put down her knitting again. "Why?"

"Luca..." Kai started then inhaled as if bolstering himself. "Luca came to me... *experienced*."

"Experienced..." Meesha repeated, her brows knitted. "Oh! He wasn't a—"

"Right," Kai answered quickly.

"Is that not allowed?"

"Normally it is, but, again, you know my father."

"Yes, a totally unreasonable male. Do you want me to speak with him? I will. I'll have no problem setting him straight. I'm not afraid of him."

Kai sat back on the couch and shook his head. "I know you aren't. But, no, the last thing we need is to get him riled up. We have two months left before the deadline."

"Yes, but the doctor said it may take six months for my body to go back to normal from the suppressants."

Kai squeezed Luca's knee. "Let's just hope it doesn't take that long."

"And if it does?" Meesha asked, looking worried.

"I don't know," Kai murmured. "Maybe I'll be able to convince him to give us more time. If not, we may have to leave the colony."

Meesha frowned. "That's extreme, isn't it?"

"For us to stay together it may be necessary. I'm not going to take another. Luca's my fated mate. And I..."

Luca held his breath.

After a long hesitation, Meesha prodded, "You?"

Kai finished with, "I don't want anyone else."

Luca's shoulders sank, and he fiddled with his tea cup. He was hoping that Kai would finally admit he loved him. He hadn't yet. Besides calling Luca "my love" that was as far as it went. Luca constantly told his alpha that he loved him. Why couldn't Kai say it back?

CHAPTER ELEVEN

Kai tried his best not to let the worry eat at him or be visible as they visited with Meesha. But he *was* worried. The doctor said there was nothing wrong with either of them from what he could see, but, even so, Luca hadn't become pregnant after three heats.

And now Luca was upset over something as he sat next to Kai on Meesha's couch. Whatever it was, Kai didn't want to bring it up in front of his former nanny.

"MeeMee, we need to go. We have a swim planned this afternoon and I want to make sure we're not out in the Great Sea when dusk falls."

A sad look crossed her face. *Bloody hell*, he was just making everyone unhappy today. He sighed.

"You just got here."

"I know. We'll come back soon. I promise. Hopefully with good news next time."

"Or you can come visit us," Luca reminded her. "I would love for you to meet my parents, too."

At least Luca had the power to turn Meesha's frown upside down.

Her face lit up when she exclaimed, "Oh, I would love to meet your parents. When are they coming in?"

Kai felt Luca's gaze land on him. He cleared his throat, ignoring his omega's stare. "They have an open invitation to visit Luca. But I assume they'll arrive for the birth of our first pup."

"Then that's another reason to get on it." She pushed to her feet and waved her hands at them in a shooing motion. "Go! Go make some babies."

No pressure. None at all.

Kai assisted Luca off the couch and after another couple rib-crushing hugs from his former nanny, they let themselves out.

On their way down her concrete walkway he glanced toward the limo. A human male was leaning back against the car, closely flanked by the two royal guards.

"Bloody hell," Kai muttered under his breath as his step stuttered.

"What's the matter?" Luca asked.

The dark-haired, handsome male with the very dark eyes had his arms crossed over his chest as he watched Luca and Kai approach.

Kai shook his head in answer to Luca, took him firmly by the elbow and led him to the car. This was one reason why he didn't come into Seaport too often. Because of run-ins with his former human lovers.

"Kai," the male greeted, tilting his head toward one guard then the other. "Will you tell them I'm not going to threaten your royal ass?"

Kai gave the guards a slight nod, and they moved far enough away to give them some space and privacy but remained close enough to protect him and Luca if need be.

"Dominic," Kai answered back.

Nic's eyes narrowed as he gave Luca a good once-over. "Is he why I haven't seen you in months?"

"Why are you here, Nic?"

Kai had to admit the man looked good and if it wasn't for Luca coming into his life, he wouldn't hesitate for even a second to go back to his place.

"I saw your fancy car parked in front of Meesha's house and I was curious as to why you've been avoiding me."

"I'm not *avoiding* you."

Nic rubbed his buttocks. "My ass says otherwise."

Luca sucked in a sharp breath next to him.

Oh great Poseidon! His omega was already upset about something Kai said in the house, and now this. This was a snag he didn't need.

"You could've told me you've moved on."

"Nic, you know there was nothing to move on from. It was..."

Nic snorted. "Casual?"

Kai pursed his lips and ignored the question. "Nic, this is Luca, my omega... *my fated mate.*" Kai emphasized the last part with the hope that Nic would pick up on what he was trying to convey.

Nic's dark eyes landed on Luca once more. "Hello, Luca. I would normally say it's nice to meet you, but now I'm out a lover. And, apparently, I can't give your prince what he needs, while you can. Lucky you." Nic pushed off the car and dropped his hands to his sides. "Though, I'm not sure how lucky you are since you have to do the job of a woman and push babies out of your ass."

"Nic," Kai growled.

Nic looked up at Kai. "Is that not true?"

"True or not, it's rude."

Nic shook his head as he studied Kai. "And it was rude that you didn't even bother to tell me."

Kai sucked in a breath. "I didn't have any obligation to tell you since you were never my only lover and you were well aware of that. But if you think I was rude, then I apologize."

Nic had been one of his favorite lovers, one of his regulars, who easily turned him on in the past. But now that he'd found his fated mate, there was no attraction at all, which surprised Kai. Nic was extremely attractive, took care of himself, and was a very experienced lover.

"You hear that, Luca? I was never his only lover. I heard he took full advantage of the king's stable of betas, as well as other... *men* in town. I'm sure he'll continue that practice once he does his duty to knock you up."

"If I'm incapable of pleasing my prince, I expect nothing less," Luca said firmly, as he pulled himself to his full height, his sea green eyes snapping.

Nic's mouth opened and then abruptly shut.

Kai pinned his lips together to keep from bursting out in laughter at his omega's sass. He motioned to his guards. "Now, if you're done trying to cause trouble, we need to go."

Nic continued to block the car door.

"Don't make my guards physically remove you, Nic."

After a long moment of the man staring Kai directly in the eye, he finally shifted out of the way. "You'll be back."

Kai shook his head. "No, I'm quite pleased with my mate," he stated as he pushed past him to open the door and usher Luca into the back seat. Luca slid all the way to the other side and Kai stopped short before following him. Instead, he shut the door and turned to face Nic. "I'm truly sorry if you thought what we were doing was anything more than rutting."

"Rutting?" Nic cocked a brow at him, a muscle ticking along his jaw. "You mean fucking?"

"You know what I mean. But, Nic, I won't have you upset my mate with your jealous actions. I won't be seeking you out in the future, I swear to that. I'm happy with the omega the fates chose for me."

"*Omega. Fates*," Nic spat. "All I hear are ridiculous excuses."

"Maybe to you they are. To our kind, they are not. It's the way things are. No matter how long we... *fucked*... I still would not have ended up with you in the end. Not that you're not a good man, though this little exchange makes me now question that, but you will find someone who wants a permanent relationship with you. It's not me. It was never me. It can never be me. I'm sorry if, for some reason, I misled you. That was not my intention."

"No, it was your intent to just get a piece of ass. I should've known that when you'd roll out of my bed and out the door every time we were finished. Not once did you stay, no matter how many times I asked."

"Again, I'm sorry if you expected more than I was willing to give. But anything we had, or you thought we had, no longer exists."

Nic tilted his head and stared up at Kai when he asked, "Do you love him?"

Kai's nostrils flared and his fingers curled into his palms. "Whether I love him or not isn't important, nor is it your business. We are fated to be together, and that's all you need to know."

"It's like an arranged marriage. It's archaic."

He was so right about that. "And now I'm done. My omega awaits me, and we have plans. Have a good day, Nic."

Before his former lover could say anything more, Kai opened the car door, slipped inside, then slammed it shut.

Luca did not look at him, instead he sat all the way on the other side of the bench seat and stared out of the window.

Within seconds, the car pulled away from the curb and Kai

refused to check to see if Nic remained where he left him. He regretted hurting Nic. Kai had taken the risk of dealing with human emotions when taking them as lovers. They tended to get attached way too easily. But they were also much better lovers than most of the betas that were at Kai's disposal, so he had thought it was worth the risk. No matter what, he was always upfront with them that their encounters would just be that and nothing more.

Nic was one lover that had always wanted more, and Kai should have broken it off a long time ago when he realized it could become a problem.

"Luca," Kai murmured. "This has been a trying day. Please don't be upset with me."

"I knew you had lovers before me. Hell, I had a lover before you."

"Then look at me."

Luca shook his head, continuing to stare out of the window as the town of Seaport flew by, his fingers digging into the leather seat of the vehicle.

"I don't know how I upset you back at Meesha's, but I wish you'd tell me what I said."

"You didn't say anything, that's the point." His omega's voice sounded thin and held a touch of hurt.

Kai's brows lowered. "What are you talking about?"

Kai watched Luca's torso lift and fall when he took a deep breath, then blew it out. "You haven't told me once that you love me."

He hadn't? Kai closed his eyes and wracked his brain to remember a time he had told Luca just that.

Maybe he hadn't.

"I thought you knew."

"I tell you all the time, my prince."

"I know. I— Oh shit. I'm not apologizing any more today. I'm all out of apologies. Look at me, Luca. Now."

When Luca finally turned, Kai couldn't miss his red-rimmed eyes. "Were you crying?"

Bloody hell, of course he'd been crying. Kai was such an idiot.

"He had feelings for you."

"Who? Nic?"

"Yes. I watched his face when you shoved me into the car, so you could speak to him without me hearing you."

"I didn't shove—"

"Kai, he had feelings for you and you totally disregarded them."

Great sea gods, this day was only getting worse.

"I didn't disregard them, Luca. He was a lover, and that was all. I never promised him more than that. I never even *hinted* at more than that."

"But he loved you. *I* love you. And you don't love either one of us. Are you incapable of feeling love?"

"Luca," Kai whispered as his chest felt as if it was caving in. "You are my fated mate—"

"That doesn't mean you love me."

"You're right, just being my fated mate does not automatically mean that I love you," Kai stated, his anger starting to boil up. "But that also doesn't mean I don't, Luca." Kai twisted in his seat to face his omega head-on. "My sire is a cold, unfeeling male. I don't even think he mourned my *pater*, even though he was the king's fated mate. I, too, wonder if he's even capable of love. If it wasn't for Meesha, I don't think I would have known what love was. Though, of course, I love my brothers. But it's not something I express with words. If that's something you need to hear, I will do better in that regard."

"I need to hear it."

The last of Kai's anger quickly fled and he grabbed Luca tightly. "Then heed me well, my omega, I love you. How can I not? How can anybody not love you, Luca? You are a kind soul.

You have accepted your fate without fighting it. In fact, you have embraced it and have made my life so much better in the short time I've known you. I wasn't in a rush to find a fated mate because I had no idea it could be this good. I truly lucked out, Luca, when you brought your light into my life."

Kai struggled to keep himself together as a mix of emotions crossed his omega's face. And when Luca sniffled...

He groaned. "Oh, please, Luca, don't start crying again unless it's happy tears. I cannot bear any more heartbreak today."

"And you won't seek out other lovers once I bear your pup?"

That brought Kai back to the conversation they'd had shortly after the Presentation Ceremony, where he had callously said he could find other lovers once he did his duty with Luca. Now he regretted every word.

"My plan is to make you happy, my mate. And, even if I had that desire, which I don't, I know that would upset you, so for that alone I would never consider it."

"But you mentioned a surrogate."

"A surrogate is not a lover, Luca, you know that. And with the king already searching for another omega, I have a feeling he wouldn't accept me taking a surrogate just to produce an heir, anyway."

Luca slid over the seat to press himself to Kai's side. Kai wrapped his fingers around the back of Luca's neck and brought their foreheads together.

A warmth radiated from Kai's belly when his omega said, "I want to have your pups, my prince."

"I want that, too," he answered softly. "I never had a desire to have pups until you, Luca. Now I want to have a dozen."

Luca pulled away, his striking green eyes wide. "A dozen?"

He kept his face neutral. "Two dozen."

"No." Luca shook his head vehemently. "Noooo."

"Three?"

"Maybe three pups in total, my prince. *Not* three dozen. "

Kai laughed. "Good, we agree on that, then."

"The most important will be the first one."

Kai's laughter died away. "No, not the most important, but as long as he's an alpha then we'll at least have my father off our backs."

"The first step is for you to plant your seed in me."

Kai's cock stirred at his words. "True." He nuzzled Luca's scent gland and inhaled deeply. "We will practice later."

"I'm already starting to get slick."

Kai glanced toward the guards in the front. With the way the tint was set up, they could see the guards through the divider, but the guards couldn't see them without Kai putting the divider down.

"We could get in a quickie if you don't push me to knot you." Kai slipped a hand into the back of Luca's pants and his omega shifted to give Kai room to work his hand down far enough to see how aroused Luca was. He slid his middle finger down his omega's crease until he found his hole. It was slippery with slick as he dipped his finger inside. Luca was open to him and clearly ready to rut.

Luca groaned against his ear. "Play with me, my alpha."

Kai pulled his hand out. "Take your pants off. Hurry." He glanced out at the passing scenery and looked for a landmark. As soon as he spotted one he said, "We have about twenty-five minutes."

"We can do a lot in twenty-five minutes."

"Not if you keep talking."

Luca snorted and, in a flash, had his shoes kicked off as well as his pants and boxers peeled down and tossed away. His hard cock jutted straight out from his naked lap and his face was flush with excitement. "How do you want me, my alpha?"

"Hands and knees, Omega. Face away from me."

Luca scrambled into position, his hands and knees planted firmly on the backseat of the limo.

Kai separated Luca's ass cheeks and shoved his face between them, inhaling his sweet, heady scent, and tasting it as well on the tip of his tongue as he circled his omega's hole. Reaching around, he cupped Luca's balls and squeezed gently before beginning to stroke his length. Luca's hips rocked back and forth, encouraging Kai to fuck him with his tongue with the same rhythm as Kai stroked his cock.

His omega tasted so good. His own erection ached and throbbed with the need to be inside his mate. The urge to plant his seed deep inside Luca was strong even though he knew it wouldn't be for anything other than pleasure.

He began to stroke Luca faster as Kai sank his teeth into his omega's luscious ass cheek.

Luca groaned. "More, my prince. Bite me again."

Kai obliged, biting the other cheek, leaving a mark there, too. Those marks would go away. Not like the one on the back of Luca's neck. When he knotted Luca during his past heats, he had held his omega down using his teeth in the flesh of his neck and it had happened so many times already that Kai thought the mark would remain.

Satisfaction ran through him at that thought. Yes, Luca was officially branded as a royal's omega. But the mark on the back of his neck was a way to show others that Luca belonged to Kai and only Kai.

Kai had caught Luca staring at the back of his neck in the mirror with a distant smile on his face, his fingers brushing over it lovingly.

In fact, it was the first time he witnessed that, he realized he loved Luca. He had just never told him outright. His mistake.

With one last circle of his tongue around his omega's wet entrance, he pulled away, scrambling to get his pants unbuckled, unzipped and pushed down far enough for his cock to be released.

He pressed a finger into Luca's hole as he stroked his own cock this time, using some of his omega's slick as lube. "Are you ready for me, my love?"

Luca's voice sounded shaky when he answered, "Yes, my alpha, I'm so ready for you. Can't you tell?"

"You always get so wet for me."

"Please hurry, my bull, take me."

Kai rose to his knees behind Luca and entered him with one forceful thrust. He dug his fingers into his omega's hips to hold him still so Kai could pound him hard and fast. Exactly how Luca liked it. How he begged for it.

"Harder, my bull."

Kai slammed his hips into Luca, giving it to him as hard as he could. The slapping sound of their skin was so loud, he was worried that the guards would overhear it and pull the car over to check on their welfare.

Suddenly Luca cried out sharply and Kai stilled instantly. "What's wrong? Did I hurt you? Am I being too rough?"

"No... my womb... it... it just opened!" His voice went from shocked to eager. "Give me your seed, my alpha."

Kai shook his head in disbelief. "Your womb can't be opening now. You're not in heat."

"It's open. I swear. I felt it."

Luca had to be imagining it. "It's not possible, Luca. You're willing it to be true."

"No, my alpha. It's happening, I swear on the almighty Poseidon. Maybe it's a false heat."

"Maybe. If it is, then your cycle is more screwed up than we thought."

"But maybe..." Luca wiggled his ass. "You need to knot me, my prince."

"I said no, Luca, we don't have time."

"Please, my bull, give me your knot. What if I'm at a fertile time even without the symptoms? We can't miss this opportunity."

"Luca, I told you not to push me to knot you in the car."

"Please, my... Kai, *please*. This could be the answer we're looking for. Please knot me and put your pup inside me. *Please*."

Kai's head spun with Luca's pleading. He wanted to make his omega happy and maybe by some fluke Luca was right. Maybe his fertile time was not aligned with his heat cycle due to the heat suppressants lingering in his system.

He glanced out of the window, trying to judge their location again. They had maybe ten minutes if they were lucky. With a groan, he leaned over, doing his best to stay connected to Luca, and pressed the button for the intercom.

"Yes, Your Highness?" came the deep voice from one of the guards.

"Take us as close as possible to the cave where our skins are kept. Once there, do not open the back doors until I advise you otherwise, do you hear me?"

"Yes, Your Highness."

With a frown, he released the button and regarded his omega still on all fours. "How is it you always get what you want?"

"You love me," Luca teased, glancing over his shoulder at Kai, his sea green eyes twinkling.

Kai pinned his lips together to keep from barking out a laugh. "You deserve a good spanking tonight."

"I know."

"I should give it to you right now. Forego the swim, forego the knot. And just smack your ass until it's cherry red."

Luca's eyelids lowered, and his mouth parted as a groan escaped. "And then you will give me your knot and afterward will take me out for a swim."

Ah, his omega thought he had Kai wrapped around his little finger. "Incorrigible urchin."

"But I'm your incorrigible urchin."

"That you are." Kai sighed in defeat. He was definitely wrapped around Luca's pinky. "You'll get your knot and your swim, then later you'll get your spanking."

Luca gave him a smirk over his shoulder, then wiggled his ass. "I'm waiting."

"Omega, you really are pushing it."

"I know, and you love every minute of it."

Kai rolled his eyes even though Luca was no longer looking at him.

Kai began to move again, slowly and gently this time. "Don't ever change, my love."

"I don't plan on it," Luca answered, then moaned when Kai hit the end of him and ground his hips.

His omega was warm and wet, his canal squeezing him tight. His scent was addictive and sometimes drove him to madness. He couldn't imagine that the bond with this male could ever be broken. By nothing. By no one.

Kai wouldn't let it.

Though he doubted that Luca was receptive to his seed, he would knot him just to please his omega. He was such a sap.

He kissed up Luca's spine, then reached around to explore the velvet silkiness of his omega's sac as he tugged on Luca's balls a little harder this time than the last. Each pull made Luca jerk against him.

"Is that too much, Omega?" Kai asked, his breath becoming shallow.

His mate started to pant also and his back arched. "No, my bull. You can never be too rough."

Kai doubted that. "So you wouldn't mind me spanking you there instead of your ass?"

Goosebumps broke out all over his mate's body. Kai began to quicken the pace of his thrusting. "*Aaah.* The thought excites you but scares you, as well, does it not?"

"It does, my bull."

"But you might not like it, and it may be the perfect way for me to punish you when you're naughty. Especially since you enjoy when I spank your ass so that ends up being no punishment at all."

Luca whimpered, and dropped his head down to the seat which lifted his ass higher. At that angle, Kai's cock slid across Luca's prostate with each slow downward stroke.

"Too slow, my bull."

"You don't get to dictate everything, Omega. I'm your alpha."

Luca gasped as Kai took shallow thrusts just to purposely tease that walnut-sized spot. "I'm going to come, my bull."

"You can't come. We have nothing to clean up the mess in here."

"But I need to come," Luca cried out.

"And I'm telling you that you must wait. You wanted my knot and you will get it. But because of that and our circumstances, you will have to wait to come."

"Then you need to stop that movement. I... *ooh*... I..."

Kai shifted enough to try to hold off Luca's ejaculation. He didn't need Luca leaving his seed all over the back of the car. He was sure the betas wouldn't enjoy cleaning up that mess.

"I'm going to come inside you, Omega, and then I'll finish you off with my mouth. Is that acceptable?"

Kai grinned as a shudder rushed through Luca.

"I thought so," Kai said, then gritted his teeth as he began to pound Luca's ass once more. Curling over his omega's back, the urge to bite Luca came over him. Except for the first night he took Luca, it normally only happened while rutting during his oestrus.

The overwhelming urge to do it when Luca was not in heat came as a surprise.

Luca cried out as Kai sank his teeth into the back of his neck. He thrust faster and faster until he felt the blood swell his cock and before he could warn Luca, he knotted him. Luca hissed and then groaned as he tightened around Kai, keeping him in place. Kai's cum filled Luca in powerful pulsating jets.

"That's it, my bull, give me everything you have. I'm so open for you. It's going to be this time, I just know it," Luca groaned.

It was impossible. If Luca couldn't get pregnant during oestrus, Kai couldn't imagine that it would work when he wasn't. He never heard of a Selkie becoming pregnant at any other time than during heat.

But he didn't want to dash Luca's hopes, so he kept his doubts to himself. He released the back of Luca's neck and licked along the indentations from his teeth left behind. Then he nuzzled Luca's scent gland behind his ear.

"We don't have much room to get comfortable to wait this out, my love. Can you bear staying as you are for a little bit?"

"A little discomfort is worth getting your knot, my alpha."

Kai once again thanked the sea gods and the fates for giving him an omega that was not only intelligent and pleasant on the eyes, but one who accepted everything thrown at him and wanted to whelp his pups. He could have very well been saddled with an unbearable omega for the rest of his life.

"I must have done something right in my life..." Kai murmured.

"What?"

"Nothing, my love." Kai sighed.

Suddenly the ride became very rough. Kai glanced out of the window and saw the guards were doing as he asked, taking them over the bluff which was a grassy but rocky incline. The king would not be happy if one of his vehicles was damaged in the process.

Kai wrapped an arm around Luca's hips to hold them tightly together, so the knot didn't pull at Luca's anus with each bump. He didn't need either of them becoming injured in those highly sensitive areas.

He sighed with relief when the car finally came to a halt and he could see the Great Sea just over the edge of the cliff they were parked along.

"I'm still hard," Luca announced matter-of-factly. "Don't let them open the doors until you do what you said you would."

Kai rolled his lips under for a moment. "They won't. Unlike you, they're good at taking orders."

"I hope so. Otherwise, we're pretty stuck in this compromising position."

"Let's just hope that this isn't a marathon knot," Kai murmured.

"Normally, I wouldn't mind, but..."

"Maybe I can move us into a sitting position?" Kai suggested, trying to figure out in his head whether it would work or not.

"Let's try that. But carefully, please."

Holding onto Luca tightly, he slowly turned them until Kai was sitting his naked ass cheeks on the leather seat and Luca sat on his lap, facing away from him.

"Better?"

Luca leaned back into Kai's chest and pressed his cheek to Kai's. "Yes, much. And now you are super deep."

Kai combed his fingers through Luca's dark blond hair. "You're going to need a cut soon."

"Mmm. You like it shorter?"

"Yes."

"Then I'll get Vin to give me a trim."

"No. Not Vin." Kai shuddered. "He's horrible with the scissors. You will end up looking like a badly sheared sheep. Marlin's beta is much better. I'll talk to Kenn. He does mine."

Luca reached back to drag his fingers along the long hair at the back of Kai's neck. "You need a cut, too. But I kind of like yours longer."

"Do you, my love?" Kai whispered into Luca's ear.

"I do. And I love when it falls across your forehead. I can picture you as a teen pup."

"I was very gangly as a teen."

"I doubt it."

"No, I was. All legs... And all alpha cock."

Luca shook with laughter. "All legs and cock. Interesting. Have you ever experimented and let another rut with you?"

Kai stilled. "What do you mean?"

"Have you ever let anyone..." Luca drifted off.

"Take me like I take you?"

Luca trailed his fingers down Kai's arm. "Mmm hmm."

"Luca, I'm an alpha."

"So? You were never curious?"

"Did that alpha let you take him?" Kai asked.

"No."

"Did you want to?"

Luca hesitated. "I wondered what it would feel like."

"I can tell you, with the right partner it's amazing and I'm sorry that you will never get to experience that. Not with me. Not with anyone."

"I thought you were all out of apologies for the day."

"Yes, you're right, but I know you're missing out on something incredible and that does deserve an apology at the least."

"So you'd never let me..."

"No, Luca. I'm your alpha. You cannot rut me. But I will take care of your little problem as soon as we untie."

"I'm not that little."

Kai chuckled and trailed his fingers up Luca's still erect cock. "No, you're not bad for an omega."

"Oh, and how many omegas have you had, my prince? I thought you had to stick to betas and humans."

"Luca..." Kai warned in a low voice.

"I'm not jealous, I'm curious."

"I've had no omegas. I'm only going by what I've heard and seen."

"Good. I want to have been your only omega."

Kai pressed a kiss to his temple. "You are. My one and only."

"I like the sound of that."

"Me, too."

"Now, how much longer do you think? I can't wait to see my prince on his knees taking care of his omega's *little problem.*"

Kai shook his head. "You have definitely earned that spanking tonight."

"I know." Luca turned his head, and they kissed and played until the knot finally released ten minutes later.

Kai ended up enjoying taking care of Luca's dilemma. And from Luca's reaction, his omega did, too.

CHAPTER TWELVE

LUCA BUMPED his head playfully against Kai's side as his alpha circled him closely in the deep blue water. The sea was a little choppier than Luca liked, but it felt so good to put on his seal skin and get out into the chilly late March water with his mate.

His excitement was hard to contain. It had been about two weeks since he and Kai rutted in the car, when his womb opened unexpectedly, but he knew. He felt it in his bones.

And the wretched puking into the toilet this morning pretty much confirmed his suspicions. He was finally carrying his alpha's pup.

But it was too soon to tell Kai. His prince still didn't think Luca was capable of getting pregnant when he wasn't in heat. Maybe the sea gods had bestowed some sort of miracle upon them.

Currently, they were about three miles out to sea and every so often, Kai would dive under the water and grab a tasty morsel to share with Luca. But after eating two small squids, Luca started to feel a little green around the glands. And he refused the third one Kai offered to him.

Kai ended up throwing it up in the air and catching it in his jaws before swallowing it down whole. Then he gave Luca a questioning look. Luca ignored it and swam away. He didn't want to get Kai excited about a possible pregnancy if Luca was wrong and had imagined everything in his desperation to remain Kai's mate.

Similar to humans, the first trimester for a Selkie was always risky for the pup. And then the whelping itself was risky for not only the pup but the *pater,* as well.

However, Luca was going to think positively. They got pregnant at a time which wasn't expected and they beat the king's deadline, so... Everything else just needed to fall into their favor, too. In nine months he would be holding Kai's pup in his arms and making his alpha bull a proud papa.

He chortled, closed his nostrils and ears, then dove under the water and spun with glee in circles through the current. When he finally surfaced, he looked around for Kai. He spotted him about a hundred yards away in a raft of seals. In all the times they had gone out swimming, they had never once come across another group of Selkies. It was surprising since the colony was full of them. It was almost as if everyone else knew to stay out of the sea, or at least at a distance, when one of the royal family was out for a swim.

Maybe it was an unspoken law.

Kai wasn't looking in his direction but was bobbing up and down in the waves as four other Selkies surrounded him. Luca immediately headed that direction, swimming as hard and as fast as he could to help his alpha in case he was in trouble. When he got closer, all the Selkies turned their large dark eyes in his direction. It didn't seem as though Kai was in any danger, but he wanted to make sure.

Kai barked at him and swam to his side, the other four following. By the bright silver of their fur, Luca realized that they were the other princes, Kai's brothers. He had no idea who was who because he'd never seen any of them in seal form yet.

The four swam with them as they took a diagonal path back toward the shoreline. Luca was glad they weren't going directly back to the cave. He could stay out in the refreshingly cool water for hours.

When he glanced up at the sun, he noticed it was getting lower, so it wouldn't be long before Kai was directing him back to the cave. But in the meantime, he was going to be the only omega out swimming with five handsome alpha Selkie princes. If his fellow omegas back in Cascadia could see him now, he was sure they would be envious.

After a half hour, the group changed direction. As they headed back toward the cave, Luca was surprised how weary he was becoming. He'd never tired this quickly before and could normally spend hours out in the sea.

The princes all still swam strongly, having no problems with the surf as they got closer to shore. But the currents kept pulling Luca away. As the distance between him and the rest of the Selkies grew, he barked loudly, calling out to Kai who was preoccupied with playing with his brothers in the water.

Suddenly, their forward motion stopped, they circled, then all five of them rushed back to Luca, encircling him. Kai nudged him with his snout and Luca let out a relieved whimper.

This unexpected loss of energy *had* to be another sign he was pregnant. In Luca's mind, there could be no other reason.

The princes all kept close—sometimes pushing him along when he struggled or simply helping to keep his head above the water when he couldn't—as they made their way more slowly back to the cave. When they reached the bottom of the stone steps, they shifted out of their seal forms, their skins hanging from their shoulders like a fur cape. Kai grabbed Luca's elbow and assisted him up the steps. But when they got to the top, he stopped Luca, a worried look in his eyes, which had returned to their Caribbean blue.

"What happened?"

"I don't know. I suddenly felt exhausted and like my flippers weighed a ton."

A muscle ticked in Kai's jaw. "I should have stuck closer to you."

Luca shook his head. "You were having fun with your brothers."

Adrian, the second oldest, had come up the steps after them and waited for the other three at the top of the narrow stairway. This was the first time that Luca not only saw them in seal form but in naked human form, as well.

Luca's eyes widened as he couldn't miss Rian's size even after coming out of the frigid water. Rian noticed where he was staring and gave him a wide grin.

Kai cleared his throat before saying, "Luca, eyes up, please."

Heat flooded Luca's cheeks. "I'm... I'm..."

"Speechless. Right?" Caol teased as he finished climbing the steps and passed them. "It figures Rian would be the one in the family with the largest cock. Lucky bastard."

"I'm not so sure anyone taking that would be so lucky," Luca responded, trying his best to keep his eyes from dropping back down to that freak of nature.

Zale, the next one to enter the cave, stopped mid-stride and then doubled over in laughter. "Oh, that was such a burn! Rian, see? No one wants that monster cock of yours. I knew it! Now you can stop bragging about it."

"I don't brag," Rian said dryly, as Marlin finally enter the cave.

"The hell you don't," Marlin scoffed, heading toward his private alcove and shaking his head.

Rian huffed. "I've never had any complaints. And I have

plenty of betas that offer themselves when I go down to their quarters."

"I bet any human male would run screaming if you whipped that out," Marlin answered, then ducked into his alcove.

"Humans? Why would I rut a human?" Rian asked in a disgusted tone.

"Are you too good for humans?" Kai asked.

"I'm a prince after all."

Kai snorted and from inside his alcove nearby, Marlin yelled, "Yes, Rian, so are we, and we've enjoyed humans and they've enjoyed us. Don't act like your cock's made of gold."

"Yes, you should try a human male sometime, Rian," Zale said, slapping Rian on the back. "They're magically delicious."

"They have no magic. They can't even shift," Rian sniffed.

Zale rolled his eyes. "You don't need them to shift, you just need them to bend over and—"

"Enough!" Kai finally yelled, his voice echoing deep into the cave. "Not in front of my omega, please."

"Luca doesn't mind. He's not a withering ninny," Caol called out as he disappeared into his own alcove. His beta servant, Beck, who had been waiting patiently by the entrance quickly followed him in to assist his prince.

"Since when did you turn into a prude, big brother?" Zale asked, his dark brows raised.

"I didn't," Kai answered. "But Luca doesn't need to hear about all your conquests. Human or otherwise."

"Have you told him about yours?" Zale said, his voice low.

"I met Nic," Luca answered, then shivered. His skin was dripping wet and he was still naked except for his seal skin which draped heavily over his shoulders.

"Ah, yes, Nic," Zale said. He tilted his head when he asked Luca, "When did you meet him?"

"A couple weeks ago, outside of Meesha's house."

Zale's head spun toward Kai. "Why did you go to Meesha's house?"

Had Kai not told them they were going to see the human doctor in Seaport?

Kai hesitated for a split second. "Just for a visit and she wanted to meet Luca."

Apparently he hadn't told them. Was it supposed to be a secret?

"And why was Nic at Meesha's house?" Zale asked Kai.

"Because he spotted the car and he wanted to have a few words."

Zale's brows rose. "I'm sure those were interesting words."

"They were," Kai confirmed, then called out to Vin. "Vin, come get Luca. Get him dried off and changed into his clothes." Kai then faced his brother once more. "Another time, Zale, yes?"

Zale studied Kai for a minute, then agreed. "You're right, it's a bit chilly in here. I need to get dressed, too. And who wants to be naked with shrinkage when Rian's striding around here with that dinosaur bone flopping between his legs?"

Luca snorted as Vin waved him over to their alcove. "Come, Luca, let me help you."

"Thank you, Vin. Has anyone told you yet today how awesome you are?"

"You just did. Thank you." Vin gave Luca a smile and a slight bow. "Now let's get this wet skin off of you, you're shivering."

———

KAI TOOK a sip of his red wine, then placed the glass on the table. That's when he realized that Luca's sat untouched. He glanced around the dinner table and noticed that everyone else was drinking. Everyone except Luca and that was not like him.

In the last four months, Kai had observed that Luca wasn't a big drinker. Most Selkies weren't. However, he still enjoyed wine with dinner.

"Do you not like that particular wine?" Kai asked in a low voice, trying not to get the attention of his brothers.

"I'm just not in the mood for wine tonight," Luca answered back.

"Do you want Ford to get you something else?"

Luca toyed with the fork that sat on the table to the left of his uneaten spinach salad. "No, I'm fine, my prince. Water's enough."

Kai frowned at Luca's salad plate. "Are you not hungry, either?"

Luca picked up his fork and poked at a cherry tomato. "I'm just still worn out from the swim."

"We'll go to bed early tonight, then."

Luca seemed to perk up at that announcement. "I look forward to that, my prince."

Kai winced when he realized everyone had been listening to their conversation and all eyes were on them.

"Luca, why do you call Kai 'my prince' all the time? Does he make you?" Caol asked from across the table. Kai also noted that Caol's wine glass was being filled by Ford for the second time of the evening.

Kai shot his youngest brother a look. "I don't force him to do anything, brother. I've told him to call me by my name numerous times. He's my mate, not my servant."

"Vin calls you Kai more than Luca does," Marlin observed. "And he *is* your servant."

"Since I don't require formalities from my own beta, that just proves that I wouldn't force Luca to call me any either, now doesn't it?"

Luca shifted in his chair next to him. "I like calling him 'my prince.'" He glanced at Caol. "Is it offensive to you?"

Caol finished chewing a mouthful of salad before answering. "No, not at all. I was just wondering. Do you call him that in the bedroom?"

Kai coughed sharply and dropped his fork to his plate. "Is that any of your business?"

"I'm curious is all."

"I call him many things in the bedroom," Luca stated.

Laughter rose up from around the table from everyone but Kai. He sighed and leaned toward his omega. "Please don't over share with these knuckleheads. They will use anything you say against me in the future."

"Yes, we will. With pleasure, too. So, what else do you call him?" Zale asked, his eyes sparkling.

Just then, Ford and Vin rushed into Rian's dining room, carrying baskets of bread and some side dishes. Even though Kai had eaten most of his salad, his stomach still growled. The swim had taken a lot out of him, too, and he was ready to replenish his body. Plus, he needed energy to pleasure his omega tonight. He enjoyed the times they rutted when Luca was not in oestrus. The rutting was less frantic and much more enjoyable, even when Luca was demanding.

It concerned him that his omega had only picked at his plate. Apparently, he wasn't the only one who noticed.

As Vin stepped up behind Luca's chair, he chided, "Luca, you have not eaten your salad. You must eat and regain your strength from your swim."

"Agreed," Kai murmured. "In all the swims we've done together in the last few months, you've never tired that quickly."

"Why is Vin hovering?" Marlin asked. "Usually the betas disappear faster than I can say 'boo' when it's not their night to cook."

"I don't know. Why don't you ask him? He has two ears," Kai answered his brother.

Marlin gave Kai a pointed look before asking, "Vin, why are you hovering behind Luca?"

"Am I, Your Highness?" Vin asked with feigned innocence and a half-hearted shrug.

"Yes, you are," Marlin confirmed. "Don't act like you don't know what you're doing."

"My prince's omega had an upset stomach this morning. I'm just here if he needs me. And to make sure he eats properly."

Kai turned to Luca in surprise. "You were sick this morning? Why didn't you tell me?"

"It was nothing," Luca said, avoiding Kai's gaze. "Vin, you can go do... whatever betas servants do when they're not needed. I'm fine. I appreciate your concern, though."

Vin made a noise, but remained where he was. Marlin was right, Vin was hovering over Kai's mate. That was not normal even for his beta servant.

He would speak to Vin privately when they returned to their own quarters, but for now, he had something to discuss with his brothers. "Speaking of concern... I'm getting worried that time's running out and father's plans to cast Luca aside and force me to take another omega mate will come to fruition."

"Yes, I heard that pest Douglass mention that father had the Seekers looking for a new mate for you. Why is he being so hard on you two?" Zale asked.

"Why does the king do anything that he does?" Marlin murmured.

"Because he can? He's the king?" Caol added.

"Because he doesn't have a caring bone in his whole body, that's why," Kai answered. "It's all about appearances to him. He has his nose shoved deeply up the Royal Council's asses."

Rian put down his glass with a thump. "Maybe he just doesn't want to see our line die out which has happened with some other royal bloodlines."

"Rian, there are five of us. *Five.* Have you not noticed that? Between all of us, the bloodline should not die out. We all love to rut." Zale shot a glance at Caol. "Some a little more recklessly than others. Even so, our father has the five of us to take his place on the throne and then he will have plenty of grandpups. I could accept that answer if he had only one son. But he doesn't, so his concern is ridiculous."

"There is a real threat, Zale, to the throne since we are all coming into our prime at the same time. Plus, omegas and pups don't always survive the whelp," Rian stated. "As we all well know, since not one of our *paters* survived."

"But we're not there yet, *Father.* There's no reason to panic," Zale reminded him. "And Kai still has a little over a month to get Luca pregnant before our sire brings down his hammer... or scepter."

"True, and I hate the pressure he's putting Kai under. I don't look forward to that," Marlin added.

"Me, neither. So you guys better produce a lot of heirs before it's my turn," Caol announced, then drained his second glass of wine, slamming the glass on the table. "Ford!" he called loudly. "More wine, please!"

"Behave, Caol. This is the dinner table, not one of the pickup joints you go to in Seaport."

"Rian, once again you have that royal scepter shoved up your royal ass. Get over it and loosen up a little. What omega will want to be mated to such a dreadful drag?"

"One that hopefully can handle that dragon between his legs," Zale said with a laugh.

"Can we not talk about my... *equipment* at the dinner table?" Rian asked, wearing a frown.

"I second that," Kai agreed.

"Of course you do, brother, because you don't want your handsome omega wishing he was a dragon slayer."

"Zale, really."

Zale eyes twinkled as he shrugged.

"Where's my wine?" Caol complained.

Rian slapped his palm on the table, making his silverware jump. "Settle down. Ford's busy preparing us dinner. If you wanted to be waited on hand and foot, you should've told Beck to come along."

Caol frowned. "This is Beck's down time."

"Which he only needs because you'll probably be using his ass as a seed receptacle later tonight. Poor Beck," Marlin murmured.

"Marlin, shut up. I give Beck a choice. I don't force him to do anything he doesn't want to do."

"He's your beta servant. Can he really say no?" Marlin asked Caol.

Their youngest brother's eyes got hard and his jaw tight. "Yes, I've made that very clear to him many times."

"Okay, enough of this conversation at the dinner table, as well," Rian barked. "Ah. Here comes Ford and Vin with the main course. Just in time."

Ford and Vin carried steaming plates of food to the table, setting each dish in front of Kai's brothers. It smelled good, but not as good as Vin's dishes. He was definitely lucky to have both Vin and Luca in his life.

Ford came behind Luca and Kai, leaned over and placed a plate in front of Kai's omega, while Vin swept away his uneaten salad.

"One of your favorites, Luca," Vin announced. "Risotto stuffed squid with a tomato, brandy and cream sauce."

Luca's chair squealed over the floor as he shoved it away from the table almost plowing into Vin. He leapt to his feet, looking green around the glands. Vin had to scramble back even more to avoid getting trampled as Luca ran from the table.

"What the—" Caol began.

"Luca!" Kai shouted as his mate disappeared around the corner.

Vin raised his hand as all of Kai's brothers pushed to their feet at once. "Please eat, Your Highnesses. I will check on him."

"Well, that was unexpected," Rian murmured as he settled back in his chair at the head of the table. He leaned forward. "Kai, are you just going to let your servant check on your omega?"

Kai scowled. "First of all, Vin is more than a servant. He's family and no, I'm going to go check on my mate." With that, Kai threw his napkin on the table and headed in the direction Luca and Vin went running off to.

Which apparently was Rian's downstairs bathroom. The door was slightly ajar and he could hear Vin murmuring something inside the room.

"Luca, what's going on?" he called out as he approached the door.

And just as quickly as Luca had fled the dinner table, the door slammed right in his face.

He jerked back and stared at it in shock. "Vin, you did not just do that!" He attempted to open the door, but his servant had locked it! "Vin, open this door."

"We're fine in here, sir. Just fine," came muffled through the thick wooden door. "Dinner didn't agree with Luca."

Kai pressed his ear to the cool wood. The sound of retching was unmistakable. "He hasn't eaten anything yet!"

"Then he drank too much sea water during your swim."

"Is that what he's ridding from his stomach? Sea water?"

A long silence greeted him, then finally a weak, "I'm fine, my alpha."

More silence, then more loud retching. Kai grimaced and placed a hand to his own stomach and swallowed down the bile that wanted to rise. Even though he wanted to turn tail and run away from seeing his omega dispelling the contents of his stomach, he knew he had to steel himself and try like crazy not to end up on his knees next to Luca sharing the same toilet bowl.

He sucked in a breath, then said, "You're not fine. Let me in. Vin! Now!"

"What's going on?" Rian asked from behind him. Kai turned and saw all his brothers gathered, watching Kai turn green himself, but also losing control of not only his omega but his beta servant! He'd never live this down.

"Vin," Kai growled. "I will leave you here with Rian and take Ford in exchange if you don't open the door right now."

"Great Poseidon, am I so bad?" Rian asked loudly.

"I'm sure Ford would love to switch with Vin," Marlin chuckled. "Poor Ford drew the beta short straw when it came time to being assigned to you."

After a few seconds, the lock clicked.

"There's your answer, Rian," Caol laughed.

Kai opened the door and saw Luca curled over the toilet, Vin on his knees next to him, petting his hair and rubbing his back in a soothing fashion.

"What the hell's going on?" Kai demanded.

Luca shakily sat back and Vin quickly wiped his mouth with a small towel. His omega turned wide, shiny eyes in Kai's direction. His skin was a pasty grey color and suddenly Kai noticed the shadows under his mate's eyes.

Why hadn't he noticed them earlier? He was a horrible alpha. "Do I need to get the doctor?" he asked more quietly.

"I think you do, brother. I think your omega's with pup," Zale answered in the doorway.

"And you know that just from him losing the contents of his stomach?"

"When was his last heat?" Caol asked.

Vin pulled a cell phone from his back pocket and tapped on the screen until he announced, "Six weeks ago."

Oh, for goodness sake, he *was* a horrible alpha. His own beta servant had been keeping track of Luca's heats. Maybe he should have been doing that instead.

"He should've been in heat again since then," Rian informed them all.

"But we just went to the..." Kai closed his eyes and sucked in a breath. He needed to come clean with his brothers. "We went to see a human doctor a couple weeks ago. He wasn't pregnant then. He hasn't come into oestrus since that visit. You all would have known if he had."

"Holy Neptune, would we ever," Caol griped.

"So it's impossible for him to be pregnant," Kai finished, raking his fingers through his hair in frustration.

"Have you rutted since his last heat?" Zale asked.

"Yes, of course, we..." Kai turned to face his brothers, his eyes wide. "Have any of you ever heard of an omega becoming pregnant at a time other than his heat cycle?"

"Brother," Rian began, "the omegas only started bearing our pups not three hundred years ago. They are still changing and evolving to help continue our race. It's evolution. Maybe in the future they won't need to wait until oestrus to be fertile. I don't know. I'm not a scientist."

"Or a doctor," Kai reminded him.

"Or a doctor, you are very right. It's just a guess. Maybe it's simply a miracle," Rian said with a shrug.

"All babies are miracles," Vin stated, still petting Luca's sweaty hair. Kai's beta wrapped his arms around his omega and pulled his head down onto his shoulder.

"I'd swear Vin is Luca's mate and not you, Kai," Zale teased.

Kai scowled at his brother. "Everybody leave us! Now!" He moved over to Luca and put a hand on Vin's shoulders. "Go call the royal doctor, make an appointment for first thing in the morning. I'm taking Luca back to our quarters."

"I'll tell Ford to wrap up your dinners. You still both need to eat something," Rian said, then disappeared from the bathroom.

"He might need to eat something bland," Zale called out to Rian. "Okay, brothers, let's leave them alone and not insult Ford by not eating his meal. I'm sure he worked hard on it."

"Be well, Luca," Marlin called out.

"I hope the best for you both," Caol said before following Marlin.

"Vin, go. I've got him."

"I'll head back to your wing, sir, call the doctor and make him some chicken broth."

Kai nodded and Vin disappeared but not before stroking Luca's hair one more time.

"I told you he would fall in love with you," Kai said gently to Luca when they were finally alone.

"I love him, too. He's been very kind to me."

"He has." Kai lowered himself to the floor and pulled Luca into his lap, wrapping his arms around his mate and cuddling him to his chest. "Did you tell him you were pregnant?"

"No. I think he's figured it out on his own."

"We don't know for sure, Luca. Again, you weren't pregnant after your last heat."

"The car..."

"You keep saying that, but I have a hard time believing it. I guess the doctor can confirm tomorrow."

Luca turned wide, red-rimmed eyes up to him. "Can we go back to the human doctor instead? I'm worried that if I'm not and he finds out my womb opened without me being in oestrus, he'll only confirm the notion to the king that I'm broken."

"Luca, you are *not* broken. Please don't say that."

Kai rocked Luca back and forth in an effort to calm his

omega's fears. "Are you feeling well enough to walk back to our wing?"

Luca nodded. "I think so. There's nothing left in my stomach for me to expel."

"You do need to eat something, though."

"I'll try. The squid from our swim turned my stomach, I think, and then when Ford placed that... dish in front of me, it just..."

"I understand."

"I'm sorry for embarrassing you."

Kai's brows lowered. "How?"

"Becoming weak during the swim and also rushing from the dinner table."

"All of that is to be expected if you're truly pregnant, my love."

"If it was some sort of false heat, how do we know this isn't some sort of false pregnancy? Maybe I'm imagining *all* of this because I'm so desperate to carry your young."

"The royal doctor can examine you tomorrow and let us know either way."

"I hope what Rian said is true. That it's some sort of miracle."

Kai pressed his lips to Luca's temple. "I do, too, Luca. You deserve to be happy."

"As do you, my alpha. And if it turns out I'm not pregnant tomorrow, maybe you should do as the king suggests and find another."

Kai lost his breath in a rush and his arms tightened around the male who snuggled against him. "Luca," he whispered, struggling to calm his spinning thoughts. "I don't want that. Ever. I've told you before and I will tell you this for eternity, *you,* Loukas of Cascadia, are my fated mate. You were chosen for me for a reason. We were meant to be together. You and I. No one else. Do you hear me?"

Luca nodded his head and shoved his face into Kai's neck. He shuddered and Kai felt his hot tears against his skin.

"Don't cry, my love."

"I can't help it," came muffled from against Kai throat. "I think it's my hormones."

Kai pressed his cheek to the top of his omega's head. "I only want you to be happy."

"And I want the same for you, Kai."

"Luca, with you in my arms, my heart, my life, I can't help but be happy."

Luca sniffled. "I love you, my alpha."

Kai's heart melted at his words. "And I you, my omega. For always."

CHAPTER THIRTEEN

"It's been about six weeks from his last heat, Dr. Harper. Luca thinks he's with pup, but he hasn't been in heat since then."

"If he's pregnant, then your omega should be six weeks along," Dr. Harper announced, pushing his glasses up his nose.

"Is there any way you can keep this to yourself and not report it to the king if he isn't pregnant?"

Dr. Harper turned his light gray eyes toward Kai. "You know I answer to your sire, Your Highness. I can't keep information as important as this from him. He wants you to produce an heir."

"It doesn't matter, anyhow, my alpha. I'm pregnant. I'm sure of it," Luca insisted. *Holy Neptune*, he hoped he was right.

"I'll be the judge of that," Dr. Harper announced and moved closer to Luca, who was perched on the examining table. The doctor pressed his cold fingers against Luca's throat and checked his pulse, then he plugged his stethoscope into his ears and listened to his heartbeat and breathing.

"One more deep breath. That's it. Fine. Everything sounds good. Have you been sleeping?"

"Yes."

"Have you been feeling queasy?"

"He's thrown up the last two mornings," Kai answered for him. "And last night, too."

Luca hated the worry that tinged Kai's voice.

Dr. Harper placed a thermometer up to his ear. "Your temp is good. Lay back on the table, Omega."

"His name is Luca," Kai growled.

Dr. Harper eyebrows shot up his forehead, then he bowed his head slightly. "Excuse me, Your Highness. Luca, please, lay back on the table."

Luca shifted back then reclined onto the paper-lined exam table. Dr. Harper opened the front of his gown and pressed his fingers along Luca's abdomen. "Any discomfort?"

"A little," Luca admitted.

"Hmm."

Hmm? What did that mean? Was that good? Bad?

"Feet in the stirrups, Luca, and please slide down to the edge of the table."

After doing what he was told, Luca's gaze fell on Kai who stood close to the table. He raised his hand and Kai immediately stepped forward to take it in his, interlacing their fingers. His alpha raised them to his lips and brushed a kiss along Luca's fingers, then held their clasped hands to his chest. Luca could feel Kai's rapid heartbeat against the back of his hand. As fast as it was pounding, he had to be just as nervous as Luca.

Dr. Harper stepped away, grabbed a squeeze bottle of something and squirted its contents onto a long wand.

Just where was *that* going?

His body trembled as the doctor stepped between his elevated feet and quickly slid the wand inside of him without a warning. Luca gasped at the invasion and swore Kai released a low growl. Luca squeezed his hand. If the doctor needed to do this to prove Luca was pregnant, then he would let him do it.

"Let me get a look-see using the ultrasound. At six weeks I should be able to see a fetus."

The doctor moved the probe around inside Luca as he studied the monitor. Kai's narrowed eyes were glued to the doctor and where the probe was inserted. His alpha was squeezing his hand so hard, it was starting to ache.

"My prince..." Luca murmured. Kai's gaze dropped to him and he loosened his grip.

After a moment, Kai asked impatiently, "Well?"

"Well..." Dr. Harper murmured. "This is fascinating."

"What is?" Kai barked.

The doctor turned the monitor to show them. Luca had no idea what he was looking at.

"And?" Kai growled, his fingers tensing in Luca's.

"I've heard about these rare cases."

"Get to the point."

The doctor pointed to a spot on the monitor. "It's very early yet. I mean, you aren't six weeks along, that's for sure. But I do see something there. You said you felt your womb open during rutting, Om— Luca?"

"Yes."

"And when was that?"

"About two weeks ago now."

Dr. Harper turned back to stare carefully at the monitor, then scratched his head. "I mean..."

"What?" Kai barked again.

The doctor pushed his glasses to the top of his head and pointed to the monitor. "I see something there. It's small. Most likely just the gestational sac. A blastocyst at most. Not quite worth mentioning at this point."

"A blastocyst? What the hell is that?"

"It's nothing more than a ball of cells that will develop into an embryo and then eventually into a fetus."

"That's my son you're talking about."

"Possibly. I mean, it's very easy for whatever it is at this point to pass through the body and never develop into anything." Dr. Harper shook his head and shifted the probe a little more. "No matter what, Your Highness, your omega's womb is closed as it should be. So if those cells are currently developing into the future heir to the throne, then everything is safe for him at this point. Your father will be pleased, Prince Kai."

"I suspect you'll still tell him even though it's too early as you say?"

"It's my obligation."

"Let me do it first. If you want to follow up with him afterward to give him the details that's fine. But I want to tell him the news," Kai insisted.

"I respect that, Your Highness. How about this... I'll give you two weeks. Bring Luca back here again right before those two weeks are up and I'll examine him once again. By that time, I may know more. I'll also run some blood work today to make sure he's healthy enough to carry the pup."

"I was already deemed healthy enough to breed before the Presentation Ceremony," Luca complained.

"But that was months ago," the doctor reminded him.

"Fine," Kai said. "I'll bring him back in two weeks. My son will be more clear on the monitor by then, correct?"

"If everything develops as it should."

"A human pregnancy test would not work, is that also correct?"

"That's true, Prince Kai. Your omega's hormonal makeup is not the same as a human female, making those over-the-counter pregnancy tests ineffective."

"A blood test?"

Dr. Harper shook his head. "It would be nice to have a simple test like that but there are not enough Selkie scientists to spend the time to develop one. They're busy working on other things, as they should be."

"Like ensuring the survival of an omega during whelp?"

"I wish they spent more time on that, as well, but again, their knowledge is already stretched thin and human scientists couldn't care less about Selkie pregnancy and whelping. I think they're afraid if we can solve those issues, then we may outbreed them."

"I'm not sure that could ever happen. The humans do like to propagate."

"That they do. But then, they still feel they're the superior race. Though we think otherwise." He chuckled and pulled his glasses back on. He suddenly got serious. "What has the timing been between your oestrus normally?"

"About four to five weeks."

"And it's been six weeks now? If you're pregnant, you won't go back into oestrus."

"Do you think the heat suppressants caused this... this misalignment of my cycles and fertile period?" Luca asked the doctor.

"Could be. But heat suppressants are a necessary evil. They can very well mess with your hormones, but it's better than becoming the *pater* to a pup with the wrong alpha, is it not?" Dr. Harper slipped the probe from him, handed him a small towel and shut off the ultrasound. "You can get dressed now. I want to see you back here in two weeks. Sooner if there are any complications."

"Thank you, doctor," Luca murmured, having a hard time pulling his gaze away from Kai.

His alpha waited until the doctor left and the door closed behind him, then he leaned down and gave Luca a long, deep kiss. Luca quickly became breathless at the unexpected passion behind it since he still laid on an examining table in a doctor's office. *And* just had a foreign object shoved up his ass.

Finally, Kai pulled away. "You were right, you are pregnant."

Luca blinked at his Alpha's matter-of-fact statement. "You heard what the d—"

Kai shook his head and assisted Luca into a sitting position. "No, my love, you're carrying my pup. I know it now. I have no doubt."

"I figured as much, but—"

"I won't ever doubt you again. You know your body better than anyone. And praise be to Poseidon, we won't have to suffer through those heat cycles for a while."

"Nine months," Luca said with a smile as he cleaned himself up. Kai's excitement was infectious.

"Yes, maybe more since you *will* be nursing my pup. No wet-nurse for us."

Luca smiled as Kai helped him off the table and pulled the gown off of him. "No, I wouldn't dream of handing our pup over to anyone else."

Kai handed him his shirt and pants. "Hurry and get dressed, I want to get you back to the castle."

"To go tell the king?"

"Great sea gods, no. It's too early yet. We'll wait the two weeks like the doctor suggested. I want to celebrate in another way... Wait, will that be safe for the pup growing inside you?"

Luca laughed. "I think so. Pregnant omegas can continue to rut. And the doctor said my womb is closed, so it should be safe."

Kai pushed Luca's trembling fingers away from the buttons he was trying to fasten and did it for him much more quickly. "Good. And after we... *celebrate*... we'll tell Vin, but he's the only one until we get confirmation from the doctor. Yes?"

"Oh yes," Luca said on a happy sigh.

Not even an hour later, Luca was laying across Kai's chest,

catching his breath, as his alpha knotted him. He loved being on top and he didn't get to do it nearly enough.

"You should let me be on top more, my prince."

"Should I?" Kai's voice was gruff and low, sending a shiver down Luca's spine.

Luca pressed his cheek against Kai's chest and let out a satisfied sigh.

"Yes. Why don't you let me do it more often?"

"Because I'm the alpha and I should be in control."

A smile pulled at Luca's lips. He deepened his voice and mocked, "I'm the alpha. I should be in control."

"Are you making fun of me?"

Luca giggled. "Yes."

Kai's body shook underneath him. Luca turned his face enough to stare up at Kai.

"I already give up way too much control to you, Omega."

"Hmm."

"Even if you are pregnant, I can still spank you for that attitude of yours."

"I didn't hear the doctor say that was acceptable, *Alpha*."

"I can call him right now and ask, *Omega*."

Luca lifted his head. "You wouldn't."

"I would."

Luca nuzzled his face into Kai's neck. "I like it, anyway."

Kai released a throaty laugh that vibrated against Luca's cheek. "I know you do."

"You wouldn't risk it."

"It's not too early to teach my unborn son some lessons in obedience."

"Lessons in obedience," Luca scoffed. "You don't want me to be obedient."

Kai brushed Luca's hair away from his face. "No. That would be boring."

Luca sighed and then pressed a kiss to Kai's chin. "I am so very happy, my prince."

Kai tucked a finger under Luca's chin and tilted his face up to plant a kiss on his lips. "Me, too."

"I hope this is the first of many royal pups that I'll be able to teach in my royal classroom."

"Yes, just don't plan on filling up that room on your own."

"You said three dozen."

"And you said three. I compromised with that reasonable number."

"Your father had five."

"With five different mates, Luca. I don't want five different mates. I don't want three different mates, either."

"Just me?"

"Just you."

Luca pressed his ear over Kai's heart. He listened to the beat of that music and smiled.

———

"Where is Loukas?" the king boomed from behind his desk in the royal library. This time Kai wasn't summoned. He had to request an audience with his own father through Douglass. He shot a frown at the beta male who flitted behind the king.

"Can you have Douglass leave us? This is private."

"You ask that every time, Kai. And when have I granted that wish?" King Solomon replied.

"How about this time?" Kai asked hopefully.

His father sighed, stared at him for a moment, then waved his hand in the air. "Douglass, please get out, but stay close in case I need you."

The pest stopped flitting and shot Kai a frown. "But, my king, you may need me close by..."

Kai scowled at Douglass who was way nosier than a servant should be. "What would he need you close by for?" Kai's growled at him. He looked at his father. "Is that twerp going to protect you from your own son?"

"No..." Solomon stopped himself before saying, "I don't have to answer that. Douglass, go." The servant's lips flattened but he reluctantly did as he was told. Then the king continued, "So, I ask again, where's Loukas?"

Kai waited for little Dougie to close the door behind him and then he faced his father. "Not here."

"Obviously. Maybe it's for the best. I have something of importance to discuss with you."

Of course he did. "And what's that?"

"I found an acceptable omega. One from a qualified family. He's been deemed fertile and goes into regular heats. His fated mate was eaten by an Orca during their bonding swim."

Kai grimaced at that news. All of it, but the graphic imagery of an Orca eating a Selkie hit him hard. They tended to play with their food before putting it out of its misery. It was one of Kai's greatest fears when they went swimming in the Great Sea. And a perfect example of why Kai refused to knot Luca in the water.

"Loukas will be cast aside and though this omega will not be your fated mate, he will do."

Just like that. The king would get rid of Kai's fated mate like he was trash. An omega who Kai loved. Simply replace him with another. Cold. Calculated. Extremely disappointing. Being a prince was certainly not all it was cracked up to be.

"I don't need another omega, Father."

"Yes, you do. Loukas isn't capable of becoming pregnant. That has become clear. It's been five months, Kai."

Kai sucked at his teeth in annoyance. This is exactly why he was facing his father alone this morning. There was no reason to upset his pregnant omega with his father's callousness. "You gave us six. Are you reneging on that?"

The king's busy eyebrows rose high. "Do you think anything will change within the next thirty days?"

"Actually, I do."

Solomon cocked a brow. "Why's that?"

Kai drew his spine ramrod straight and announced with pleasure, "Because Luca is now carrying my pup." He followed it with a great big smile.

The king sat back in his gaudy gilded chair and studied Kai with his midnight blue eyes. "How is that possible? Did he have a heat I wasn't informed about?"

"No."

"Then it's impossible."

"I thought that, too, but Dr. Harper will confirm it with you. So no other omega is needed. I carried out my duty by producing an heir and Luca's the one carrying him."

The king steepled his fingers in front of his face, tapping his index fingers together. After a long moment he dropped his hands and placed them firmly on his desk. Leaning forward, he narrowed his gaze on his oldest son. "My other requirement, my son, in case you have forgotten, was a surviving alpha pup. I will still have that omega brought in, just in case Loukas is incapable of producing an alpha."

Kai's smile dropped like a deflated balloon.

Since alphas apparently ran strong in the king's bloodline that shouldn't be a problem, so why was his father bringing that up? Did he think Luca's bloodline would be the weak link in producing alphas?

"Must every Selkie in line for the throne be an alpha?"

Solomon's chin jerked back. "Do I really need to answer that?"

No, his father didn't need to answer that. Kai knew that was true. The Royal Council would never accept a beta or omega king, which meant they couldn't become a prince, either. They couldn't even hold any royal title at all. Only an alpha could rule a colony. It was law.

Law. Kai grimaced.

Hundreds of years ago if an alpha was not the firstborn son of a fated mate, the family would destroy the pup's seal skin and then drown the newborn in the sea. More often than not, they would do the same to the fated mate, declaring they were flawed.

King Solomon had produced five living alpha pups. Though, now that Kai thought about it, he had no idea what gender the pups were that didn't survive. Had they been alphas, as well? Or had his father followed the ancient tradition of throwing any of his beta or omega offspring into the sea to perish? He'd been told that all his half-siblings who hadn't survived had died during their whelp, and Kai never questioned it.

But maybe he should have.

What was also strange was that the king had lost five omegas. That was a lot for one alpha to lose. Especially one of royalty who would have the means to provide better medical care to his whelping omegas than the common folk.

Could his father be so cruel by ridding himself of any pups that weren't alphas and any omegas who didn't produce alphas?

This might be why he was pushing Kai to take another omega, one whose family was most likely known to produce alphas. Maybe the king had discovered Luca's line was more apt to produce omegas than alphas.

Even so, Kai didn't know any Selkie families that followed that barbaric practice anymore, thanks be to Poseidon. But royal expectations were a much higher than the common folks'. And King Solomon was... well... King Solomon.

"Douglass!" the king yelled out.

Immediately the door opened, making Kai wonder if the weasel had his ear glued to the door the whole time.

"Congratulations are in order, Your Highness," Douglass said as he rushed to the king's side.

Aaaaand that confirmed it. He was not only a weasel but a nosy one at that.

"Call—"

"Already done, sire. Dr. Harper's on his way."

"I want Loukas to see the doctor once a week to make sure everything is going smoothly." Solomon turned his head toward Douglass. "Make sure I get a weekly report."

Dougie bobbed his head up and down with enthusiasm, probably like he did when he sucked the king's—

"Once a week is excessive, Father."

"Not for a possible future king."

"To make him king both you and I would have to die. And you're way too stubborn to do that." With that Kai tilted his head in a curt farewell and spun on his heels. He couldn't get out of that library fast enough.

CHAPTER FOURTEEN

"Why would he do this?" Luca cried, the tears streaking his cheeks. He was squeezing the pint of mint chocolate chip ice cream so hard, one side of it was crushed in and the contents were starting to squeeze over the top. He jammed the spoon into the container, took a big scoop and then shoved it back into his mouth.

Kai sighed as he stared at his omega sitting in the middle of his bed, falling apart emotionally.

These emotional meltdowns were happening way too often now.

Pregnancy was not all it was cracked up to be. Just like being a prince. Kai had no idea what he had done to deserve either of them.

"My son needs more than ice cream to help him grow, my love," Kai said with contrived patience.

Luca licked the spoon clean then stabbed it into the container again. "I like ice cream."

"I know. The freezer is jammed packed with it. Vin's coddling you too much."

Luca dropped his hand to his rounded belly which peeked out from the bottom of the ill-fitting T-shirt. And it wasn't even Luca's shirt, it was Kai's who was a size larger than Luca. "I can't help it if your son makes me crave ice cream."

"And chocolate."

"And chocolate!" Luca exclaimed loudly, brandishing his spoon in the air.

"And mashed potatoes."

"Yes, mashed potatoes!" Luca groaned. "Can you ask Vin to boil some potatoes? Lots of butter, please. And some sour cream. No lumps."

"Luca, really."

His omega grunted and shoved another spoonful of the frozen green dessert into his mouth.

He wouldn't put it past Luca to bite him if Kai tried to wrestle the spoon away. Instead he decided on another tactic. "Would you like to go for a swim?"

Luca's mouth dropped open, and he stared at Kai in horror. "I can't fit in my seal skin! You know that!"

Oh holy sea gods. Kai just stepped in it again. "It will stretch somewhat," he suggested carefully.

"Not enough. Not anymore. I'm way too fat for it. I'll get out there looking like a... a whale!" Fresh tears poured from his omega's constantly leaking eyes.

"You look nothing like a whale. You're much more handsome than that."

"My face is pudgy. My feet are swollen."

"You're perfect."

"You're just buttering me up. Did I mention to put loads of butter on the mashed potatoes? Why doesn't he send that omega away?"

Kai inhaled a deep breath and moved to the bed where the sheets were in a tangled mess that resembled a circle. It was almost as if Luca kept trying to nest in their bedding. Most mornings Kai woke up without even a corner of the sheet covering him. He'd looked over and see Luca cocooned in not only the sheets, but he also stole all the pillows during the night, tucking them around his protruding belly.

Kai sank his weight on the edge of the bed and held out his hand.

With reluctance, Luca passed him the container and the spoon. Kai placed it on the nightstand and after kicking off his shoes, climbed into bed, taking his omega into his arms.

And, of course, that set off fresh water works.

"How can you have any tears left?"

"I don't know. I don't want to cry. It just happens!"

Kai pulled him close, wiped away a bit of ice cream from the corner of Luca's mouth with his thumb, then placed his hand over the bump that housed his unborn son. "How's he doing?"

"He's active today. I swear he's been kicking my bladder all morning."

"Then he'll be a good swimmer."

"All Selkies are good swimmers, my prince."

"Ours will be the best."

Luca snorted then wiped at his tears. "What if he's not an alpha?"

"He will be," Kai assured him, though he secretly wondered the same thing.

"And if he's not?" Luca prodded.

"Then, once again, I'll be prepared to leave, to give up my station here to build a life with you elsewhere."

"You would do that for me?" Luca blubbered.

"Luca, yes. But it's not just you now, it would be for our son, too." He rubbed Luca's belly softly, hoping to feel some movement. "He's not so active right now. You probably gave him brain freeze with all that ice cream." Luca gave a little laugh that pulled a smile from Kai. "You need more laughter and fewer tears."

"How can I not cry when there's an omega waiting in the wings for my fated mate? Have you met him?"

Oh, good gods. His answer was going to start another flood of tears. But he didn't want to lie to Luca. "Yes."

"I want to meet him."

"There's no point."

"But he could be my replacement. I want to make sure he's good enough for you, my alpha." A snot bubble escaped Luca's nose as he burst out in tears again.

Kai made a noise, grabbed a tissue off the nightstand and wiped Luca's face. "You're not being replaced."

"But you have obligations..."

"Yes, to you and... and... Junior."

Luca's tears came to an abrupt halt, and he sat up straight, his red-rimmed sea green eyes narrowing. "We're not naming him Junior."

Kai smirked. "I kind of like it."

"No."

"Yes, I'm the alpha and I'll decide on his name."

Luca shook his head. "Oh no."

"Yes, Omega, you must obey me."

Luca snorted. "Since when?"

"Since the day we bonded."

"I must have forgotten to read that royal memo."

"You must have," Kai murmured. "Now, my love, lie back on the bed and let me speak to my son in private."

Kai propped pillows behind Luca's dark blond head and then slid down the bed, putting his mouth close to Luca's belly. He pushed the tight shirt up so his pup could hear him clearly.

"Hi, Junior, it's your father..."

"Kai, he will not be named Junior!"

Kai glanced up at his mate. "This is a private conversation." He turned back to Luca's belly. "Your *pater* is being very unreasonable right now. I want to name you Junior and he doesn't agree. He's very disobedient. I'm going to tally up all the spankings he's earned for the past few months and give them all to him after you're whelped. His ass will be a bright red when I'm through."

"You will not."

"Hush, Omega."

Luca's belly shook.

Kai cocked a brow in Luca's direction. "Are you finding this funny?"

"No. Carry on with your conversation with my son," Luca commanded.

"Our son."

"My son who will *not* be named Junior."

"Junior, listen... I'll apologize in advance since stubbornness runs in both sides of your bloodline. You're probably going to be a stubborn little brat..."

"Kai!"

Kai snorted. "But we'll love you anyway."

"Mmm hmm."

Kai pressed a kiss to Luca's belly. "Maybe we should name you Lucky since I can't believe how lucky I am to have not only you but your *pater*. There can't be a luckier Selkie in existence than me."

"Really?" Luca exclaimed.

"You don't believe me?"

"No, about the name Lucky. Our pup will not be Lucky *or* Junior. The king would have a coronary."

"Then that settles it. Lucky it is."

"Kai!"

Leaving a hand on Luca's belly, he shifted up the bed to lay by his omega's side, pressing a kiss to his temple. "Then name our son."

"Now?"

"Yes, why not?"

Luca gave him the side eye. "Why? Because I might not survive the whelp?"

Kai sucked in a sharp breath. "Luca, don't even say that."

"But it's something to think about. What will you do if I don't? What if I don't survive and our son does? Will you raise him by yourself? Or take that omega that's waiting in the wings, so he can step in as *pater*?"

"I'm not going to even entertain those thoughts."

"But you must, my prince. You must. You must be ready in case... In case, one or both of us doesn't make it."

"Luca, stop it. We'll not only have the midwife but both the royal doctor and the human doctor. I've already made the arrangements."

"And a wet-nurse on standby."

"Again, stop. You *will* be nursing our pup."

"I hope so." Luca reached up and brushed a lock of hair off Kai's forehead. "Do you know what I crave more than mint chocolate chip ice cream right now?"

"Pickles?"

Luca thought about that for a moment, then shook his head. "No. You."

"Your pregnancy has been nothing but tears, eating and rutting, my love. Is that normal?"

Luca shrugged. "Hormones."

"I guess I can sacrifice myself for the cause."

"The cause?"

"Of making you happy. I keep the freezer stuffed full of ice cream and you stuffed full of me."

Luca smiled. "Yes. That makes me happy."

"But," Kai raised a finger, "you must promise not to bawl your eyes out like last night when we rutted."

"It was tender and loving and... very emotional."

"That's because I don't want to be rough right now for obvious reasons."

"Dr. Harper said it was safe."

"Yes, it was safe to rut, but you didn't inform him how insatiable you are."

Luca grinned. "No."

"So it will be tender and loving for the next month no matter how much you beg otherwise."

Luca pouted. "Then be prepared for me to soak the bed."

"With slick?"

"No, with my tears."

Kai, his lips pinned together to keep from laughing, rolled off the bed and stripped himself of his clothes.

When he was naked, he stared at Luca who just sat in the middle of the bed staring back. "Are you just going to sit there or are you going to get undressed?"

His omega whipped off his shirt and threw it in Kai's face.

"Is that any way to treat a prince?" Kai teased.

"Only if he's my prince." Luca wiggled on the bed. "You may have to help me with my boxers."

Kai stroked his now raging erection. Never in a million years did he think seeing his omega heavy with his pup would turn him on. But it did. They might have to rethink only having three and go back to planning three dozen. Kai loved seeing Luca's belly stretched due to the growing life inside him.

They made that new life together. Just the two of them. They created something that would be a piece of them both.

Color rose into Luca's cheeks as he attempted to cover his expanded belly with his hands, a worried look on his face. "Am I not attractive anymore?"

"No, just the opposite, my omega. Being pregnant with my son makes you glow."

Relief wiped away Luca's look of doubt. "Does it?" Then he got a naughty twinkle in his eyes. "I bet I'll be really radiant once you knot me."

Kai dropped his head to stare at his bare toes and shook his head. "You are something else."

"I know. You love it."

"I do. Another alpha might not tolerate your impudence."

"I'll never have to worry about that."

"No, you won't."

"So come help me take off my boxers, my bull. I need you inside me."

Kai needed that, too. "Are you sure it's not too crowded in there already?"

"No. My bull, you must hurry. I'm leaking on the bed."

"Then we will have Vin change the sheets afterward. I'm not rushing tonight." Kai climbed onto the bed and in between Luca's legs. He tugged his omega's boxers down enough so his cock sprung free.

"Is it still there?" Luca asked, lifting his head to peer down his body.

"What?"

"My cock. I haven't seen it in so long."

"Yes, it's there. Let me check a little closer to make sure it's still working properly..."

Luca let out a long, low groan as Kai wrapped his lips around his omega's erection, sucking him hard. After licking the length, he circled the sensitive head. Luca's fingers dug into Kai's hair, attempting to control Kai's pace.

"Oh, that feels so good, my bull. Your mouth... *Ah... Kai...*" Then a loud sob escaped Luca.

Kai released him and lifted his head to look over Luca's very large belly. "If you cry, I will stop."

Luca nodded, sniffling. "Okay, I won't cry. I promise."

Kai rolled his eyes at that fib and took Luca back into his mouth, tracing the edge of his cock's crown with the tip of his tongue. He cupped Luca's balls and his fingers playing gently along the velvety soft sack of skin. He squeezed slightly, then sucked Luca's length deeper into his mouth.

"Oooh, that's it, my bull. That's it... It won't take me long... It won't take..." Luca's fingers twisted so tightly in Kai's hair that his eyes watered from the pain. But even so, Kai didn't let up. He bobbed his head up and down Luca's cock, teasing, sucking, licking, tasting the salty precum that was leaking at a rapid rate. He slipped his fingers down to Luca's hole to confirm his slick was leaking just as quickly.

Kai groaned around Luca's length as he slipped a couple fingers inside his mate and, finding his prostate, began to stroke it.

"Oooh... Oooh. Great sea gods! My alpha... I'm going to—"

Hot, salty jets of cum pulsed from Luca's cock down Kai's throat. He didn't waste a drop and once Luca stopped throbbing in Kai's mouth, he released him and moved until he could see his mate's flushed face, parted lips and closed eyes.

"Good?" Kai asked him with a grin, already knowing the answer from Luca's blissful expression.

"The best," breathed Luca.

"What do you want now, Omega?"

Luca's eyes fluttered open, and he gave Kai a wide satisfied smile. At least he wasn't bawling.

Yet.

"Your knot."

Of course. Kai expected no other answer, but it still turned him on to hear it. "How do you want it? Side or back?"

Without even a hesitation, Luca answered, "Like I am now. I

want to see my prince's handsome face when he fills me up with his seed."

"Spread your legs wider, Omega."

Luca shifted his hips and did as he was told.

Kai leaned down and placed a kiss on the top of Luca's belly. "Just ignore us, my son. Your parents are a randy couple and your *pater* likes to get loud, so you might want to close your ears."

Luca chuckled. "Give me a kiss, my bull."

"I taste like you," Kai warned him.

"I don't care."

Kai carefully leaned over and took Luca's mouth, teasing his omega's tongue with his. He brushed his thumbs over Luca's nipples, swallowing his gasp and taking the kiss deeper.

After a moment, Kai pulled away enough to say, "I love you very much, my bringer of light," against Luca's lips.

"And I you," his mate answered. "Now, take me and don't forget to play with my nipples when you do so. They are so wonderfully sensitive right now."

"Let me know if it gets to be too much."

Luca just smiled. Nothing that Kai had ever done to Luca had been too much. Everything Kai gave, Luca took and asked for more. Kai shook his head, shifted forward, remaining on his knees to keep his weight off Luca's belly, and aligned the swollen head of his cock with his omega's slick hole.

"Are you ready?"

"Always."

And that was the truth. His omega never said no. He could never get enough of rutting with Kai. But it was mutual.

A hiss escaped Luca's lips as Kai pressed forward, taking him slowly. "Yesss, my bull, make me yours."

"You're mine. You'll always be mine, Luca. No one else's."

Luca's eyelids fluttered closed, and he panted as Kai began to move, his hips keeping a slow, steady rhythm until Luca squeezed tightly around him. The feeling of being inside his mate was a mix of both heaven and home.

"I don't want to knot you yet. I'm enjoying this too much." Kai didn't want to rush this. Soon they would need to stop rutting and wait until after their son was born. Even after that he knew there would be a recovery time. So, he wanted to take his time and make this last.

Kai leaned over again and sucked one of Luca's nipples into his mouth. Luca cried out and clenched around Kai's cock even tighter. He blew out a breath then teased Luca's other nipple with the tip of his tongue, circling and flicking, then he sucked it hard.

Luca cried out, his back arching slightly. "More..."

As Kai sucked even harder, he increased the pace of his hips as he thrust as deep as he felt was safe.

Luca's fingers clawed down Kai's back, digging into his flesh, as he encouraged Kai to go faster. Kai released Luca's nipple and grunted. It took every effort he had not to do as Luca wished.

Kai shoved his face into Luca's throat and sank his teeth into his neck. Luca's groan vibrated against Kai, making the blood rush into his cock, swelling it even larger. Kai grunted again as his knot expanded and it tied the two of them together, his cock throbbing intensely as pulses of cum shot deep into his omega.

After a moment, Kai released Luca's neck and pulled away, so he wouldn't risk putting any of his weight on Luca's ever-growing stomach.

"You okay?" Kai panted, as his cock twitched a couple more times deep inside Luca.

"Oh yes."

"Prop the pillows behind you. That's it." Kai sighed. "This may be the last time, Luca," he warned.

Luca's green eyes went wide. "No!"

"Yes, just until after the pup is whelped. I worry—"

"I still have a month to go," Luca argued.

"I know, but—"

Luca cut him off. "I'll get a doctor's note."

"Luca, really."

"It's fine."

"I'll talk to the doctor myself."

"And he'll tell you it's safe," Luca insisted.

"We'll see. You feel no discomfort at all?"

"This whole pregnancy is one big discomfort. But, no, nothing that bothers me enough to stop us from rutting."

Kai sighed.

Luca's eyes narrowed. "I thought you didn't want me to cry during our rutting tonight?"

"I didn't... I don't."

"Then don't speak of holding out on me or I'll start to bawl. And I won't stop until you give in."

Kai snorted at his mate's attempt at blackmail. "If the doctor confirms it's safe during the last month, I won't withhold it from you, okay?"

"Promise?

Kai brushed Luca's hair out of his face and whispered, "Promise." He frowned. "Hard to cuddle with you during the knot when we're like this."

Luca patted his belly. "Someone's in the way."

"I should've thought of that beforehand."

"I wanted to see your face."

Kai arched a brow at him. "Well, now you're stuck looking at it for the next five to ten minutes."

"I'll never get tired of looking at you, my prince." Luca held his gaze for a second then a pensive expression crossed his face and his sea green eyes widened once more as his mouth gaped open.

"What's wrong?"

"Son of the sea," his omega whispered.

"What?"

"Son of the sea," Luca repeated. "Dylan."

It took Kai a few seconds to realized what Luca was talking about. He was naming their son Dylan. His heart swelled in his chest. "That's a good strong alpha name. You chose well."

It was perfect. The name was fitting for a future prince.

Luca shrugged. "It just came to me."

"I'm surprised it did with your 'baby brain.'"

"What does *that* mean?"

Kai schooled his expression. "Nothing," he said quickly.

"Do you think my brain has been mush? Am I forgetful?"

"No, you're definitely *not* forgetful."

"That's right, I can't forget your father has that omega just hanging around waiting."

Kai sighed. "Luca, please. Will you drop it?"

"How can I? Would you like it if I had an alpha on standby? Just in case?"

"My love, we're still knotted here. We're supposed to be enjoying the afterglow of our beautiful coupling and you want to talk about someone else."

"Someone else who's waiting for me to fail."

"Luca, how about this... As soon as Dylan's born, I'll insist my father send that omega away if that will make you feel better."

"But you've talked with him." It wasn't a question; it was an accusation.

Oh, here we go again.

"Yes, I have. Only to be polite since he traveled a long way, my love. It's not his fault that I don't have eyes for anyone but my bonded mate who carries my pup."

Kai held his breath and waited. He wasn't sure what to expect next from his mate. His emotions were like the changing tides of the Great Sea. Luca could either smile in satisfaction at

Kai's words or produce a bucket of tears. The odds tended to lean towards the bucket.

Kai was surprised when his omega did neither. Instead Luca looked thoughtful when he said, "I actually feel sorry for him."

Kai lifted his head. "Why?"

"Because he will never have you, my prince. He'll be missing out on an extraordinary love."

"Luca," Kai breathed, his heart skipping a beat.

Luca intertwined their fingers and placed their hands on top of his belly. "It's true. Oh! Did you feel that? Dylan's spinning circles in there."

Kai flattened the palm of his free hand on the side of Luca's stomach, which was moving with each kick of their pup. "Yes, I feel him. He's happy."

"He's eager to meet us."

"Just as we are to meet him. But he has another month," Kai reminded him.

"Dylan, you heard your father. Have some patience, we'll all be together soon."

Just then, Kai's knot released, and he slipped to Luca's side to gather him into his arms. "Soon." He turned them until they were spooning, Kai's hands remaining on Luca's stomach so he wouldn't miss one little movement of his unborn pup. "Have you spoken to your parents?"

"Yes. They'll be here in two weeks. They don't want to miss the whelp. And they're also very anxious to meet you."

"I'm sure. And I can't wait to meet them. I plan on thanking them profusely for bringing such a wonderful male into the world."

"Kai," Luca whispered as his body lurched once again with a sob.

"Oh bloody hell, Luca! Your tears could flood the Great Sea."

Luca chuckled through his tears. "Well, stop saying such loving things."

"Never."

Luca reached back and cupped Kai's cheek. "Then I will need to find something that makes *you* weep with emotion."

Kai circled his palm over the tight skin of Luca's belly. "I don't think that will be hard to find."

"I love you, Kai."

"And I you, Luca."

EPILOGUE

"It's time!"

Kai glanced up from his desk where he was writing a petition to the Royal Council, trying to convince them to do away with the branding of royal omegas.

"Time for what? It's too early for dinner."

"Kai, it's *time!*" Caol yelled impatiently.

Kai shot to his feet, knocking his chair to the floor behind him with a clatter. "How do you know?"

"Because Vin just about bit my head off when I asked him the same question."

"Great Poseidon! Luca's in whelp?"

"No. It's time for his massage. Of course, he's in whelp!" Caol shouted even louder from the doorway to Kai's study.

"Where is he?"

"Last I saw, Vin was rushing him down to the whelping pool."

Kai's head spun. He didn't know what to do first. "Luca's parents!"

"Zale went to get them."

"The midwife!" Kai spouted.

"Rian."

"Dr. Harper."

"Marlin."

"The human doctor!"

"Meesha is bringing him."

Kai frowned. "How does she know?"

Caol rolled his eyes. "I called her."

"Wait! Did everyone know before me?"

"Seems so."

"Well, that's not right," Kai grumbled.

"What's not right is you're still standing there. Let's go!"

Shit!

"Caol," Kai said, his feet still not moving.

"What?"

"Dylan's coming."

"I know."

Kai shouted, "No, Caol! Dylan's coming!"

"I know!" Caol shouted back. "And if you want to be there, you'd better hurry!"

When Caol turned tail and disappeared, Kai strode out of the room. Once he hit the corridor outside his quarters, he began to jog. As he hit the open air, he broke into a sprint over the bluff, heading toward the cave that held the whelping pool.

His heir, his firstborn son, was on his way.

———

Kai doubled over, out of breath. "Thank the gracious sea gods!" burst from him as he saw that not only the midwife was on hand but also both doctors. Meesha was kneeling next to the salt-water pool with what looked like a death-grip on Luca's hand.

Even though his mate was submerged up to his shoulders in the pool that had been chiseled into the cold stone, sweat beaded on Luca's forehead.

Kai rushed to the edge and the colony's midwife looked up in surprise. "Sire, a male of your station does not attend the birth of your own pups."

Kai's spine stiffened, and he gave the male a scowl. "Since when do you dictate the rules to your prince?"

The midwife bowed his head. "I'm sorry, Your highness. It appears that I've overstepped my boundaries. I hoped to help you avoid the ire of our king."

Now Kai felt bad. He had pulled rank on a male who was only there to help Luca during the whelp of their son. He tilted his head in apology and said in a much gentler tone, "You let me worry about that."

"Yes, Your Highness."

Kai went to his knees near Luca's head. "How are you?"

Luca glanced up at him his face tight, his green eyes dark as they reflected the discomfort Kai was sure he was feeling. "I'm ready to meet our son."

"Soon, my love." He glanced at the doctors who stood nearby, ready to assist the midwife if need be. "Someone hand me a cloth."

By the time he lifted his hand, a washcloth appeared in it. Kai folded it up and dabbed the sweat off Luca's forehead. "Is it very painful?"

"Not yet."

Kai eyeballed the midwife. "How long does this normally take?"

"Your Highness, it all depends. Each omega is different. However, Dr. Harper examined Luca before he entered the pool and his womb is opening so that's a good sign."

Kai nodded. Luca's clenched his teeth and whimpered.

"What is it?"

"A contraction," Meesha informed him. "They seem to be coming pretty quickly. But I know nothing about Selkie births."

Neither did Kai. He should have studied up on them. Once again, he failed his omega.

"Where are my parents?" Luca asked when the contraction subsided.

"Just outside the cave. They're waiting with my brothers," Kai assured his mate.

"Are all your brothers out there?"

Kai smiled. "Yes, they're all excited to meet their new nephew."

"I can't fail them," Luca whispered.

"You won't fail them."

"Dylan must survive, and he has to be an alpha. He must be, my prince. Otherwise, I've failed."

"Never. Dylan just must arrive healthy and you must remain so, as well. That's all that's expected."

"From you, but not your father."

"And who's your mate?"

"You."

"So who matters the most?"

"You," Luca repeated, then grimaced as another contraction made his body tense.

Kai looked at the midwife. "Is there anything you can do?"

"You and Miss Meesha are doing it, Your Highness. Just keep him occupied and hold his hand. We'll step in when needed, but it's best to let nature run its course."

Nature? Omegas have only been giving birth for approximately three hundred years. There was nothing natural about it. That's why so many died during whelp. But Kai bit his tongue. There was no reason to voice his worry, it would only make Luca upset.

An hour later, Kai was as sweaty as Luca as the contractions came only a minute apart. He couldn't take any more of Luca's screams as the pain wracked his body.

"Is there nothing you can give him?"

"It's not advisable, Your Highness," the midwife said. He was now in the pool with Luca, waiting as the time got closer.

Kai pushed to his feet and began to strip off his clothes. Meesha gave him wide eyes. "What are you doing?"

"Getting in with him."

"Prince Kai," Dr. Harper began.

Kai raised his hand. "No. I'm getting in the pool with my omega and you all have no say." He finished undressing and slipped in behind Luca, so his mate was settled between his legs.

Kai stroked Luca's damp hair with one hand and his belly with the other. "Lean back on me, my love. I'm here with you. I wish I could take the pain from you."

Luca shook his head. "No. It's my job to whelp your sons. I need to remain strong."

"You're very strong, Luca. Don't ever doubt that."

Luca leaned his head back on Kai's shoulder, but that was short-lived. Another contraction had him sitting up and panting through the pain.

"I think he's almost here, Luca. Not much longer," the midwife assured Kai's mate. "I'm going to check to see if he's crowning yet, is that okay with you?"

Luca nodded, and answered, "Yes," through clenched teeth.

The midwife's hands disappeared under the water.

"Are all Selkies born in the water?" Meesha asked as she perched next to the pool.

"Yes, to ensure they're born with their seal skins. If they aren't, they won't survive."

"Do most colonies have whelping pools?"

"No, some still whelp the old fashion way out in the sea, but that leaves the *pater* and pup very vulnerable to predators. Some of the omegas in our colony prefer to do it the natural way, as well, but it's their choice. All have access to the whelping pool."

"Humans give birth in water, too, sometimes," she murmured.

"Is it easier on them?"

Meesha shrugged, her eyes holding sadness. "I don't know. I didn't have the option when my own son was born."

Kai reached up and grabbed Meesha's free hand. "I'm sorry you had to go through that loss, MeeMee."

"You filled in a hole I never thought would be filled again. I'm grateful to you, Kai. And I'm also thankful that you brought Luca and soon your own son into my life. My heart's full."

Kai gave her a smile. "Your generosity and selflessness made me a better person. And I thank you for that."

The midwife interrupted them. "He's coming, Your Highness, I feel his head crowning."

Luca groaned and then cried out as another contraction ripped through him.

"Hang on, my love, our son's almost here."

"Push, Luca," the midwife encouraged. "*Push.*"

Luca leaned forward and, with a growl, pushed and then screamed.

Suddenly everything happened at once. Luca cried out Kai's name, the midwife grabbed at something between Luca's legs, and Kai spotted the whitest fur he'd ever seen just under the water.

And then he saw nothing because his eyes were full of unshed tears.

———

"Your Royal Highness, I present to you Prince Dylan of the

North. Firstborn son of Prince Kai of the North and his omega, Loukas of Cascadia."

Kai did everything in his power not to swat Douglass away from him. He was fluttering around them like a blood-thirsty mosquito. And instead of announcing the newest heir to the king with pride in his voice, the pest sounded somewhat bitter.

Kai had no idea why. But he'd had just about enough with his father's personal assistant. The beta forgot his place time and time again. However, Kai had to remind himself that now was not the time to deal with it. No. Now was the time for more pomp and bloody circumstance.

Kai glanced down at the baby in his arms. Dylan had a shock of dark hair and his pudgy little legs kicked wildly. He was impatient just like his father. Caribbean blue eyes, also just like his proud father, stared up at him as his son complained in a way only an infant could.

"If he's fussy, I can take him," Luca said under his breath as he stood by Kai's side.

Both were dressed in what was considered royal garb and even the blanket wrapped around Dylan seemed to be spun in gold. Though, Kai doubted it was. If it had been up to Meesha, his son would have been wrapped in one of the numerous knitted baby blankets she had given them. He swore there would be one for each of the three dozen sons he threatened Luca with.

"I have him. If we don't follow these damn traditions, we'll be here longer than we need to be. I just want this to be over."

"I as well, my prince. I think Dylan needs to be fed and I'm starting to leak."

Kai cocked a brow and Luca stifled a laugh.

Caol leaned forward and whispered. "Did Luca say leak?"

Kai ignored his youngest brother.

Luca did also, since he continued as if his four brothers weren't standing behind them, all within hearing distance. "Not the same type of leak as the first time we met in this hall, my virile alpha bull. I'm leaking milk this time."

Marlin snorted and repeated, "Virile alpha bull?"

Douglass shot them all an annoyed frown.

Kai opened his mouth to answer, but he was interrupted by his father's booming voice as he addressed the royal doctor, who stood at the foot of the throne.

"He's an alpha?"

"He is, Your Highness."

"Healthy?"

Dr. Harper tilted his head. "Yes, sire."

King Solomon's busy brows dropped low. "Is his fur silver?"

Great Poseidon! Was being an alpha and healthy not enough for his father? Was the male still looking for an excuse to rid Kai of his fated mate? To find the most minute fault?

Kai was about to tell his father that he could shove his royal scepter up his ass when Dr. Harper continued.

"It is currently still white, Your Highness, which is normal at that age, but has the promise of turning silver."

"Father—" Kai began.

"You have done well, my son, Prince Kai of the North. Upon my demise, you are next in line for this throne. Upon yours, your son, Prince Dylan of the North will reign. This will ensure the continued success of the Northern Colony for generations to come."

"He acts like I've saved the race or something," Kai muttered.

"Or something," Zale whispered back. "At least you've taken the pressure off the rest of us."

"Don't count on it," Kai murmured.

"Now," the king boomed from his throne. "The Seekers will

be instructed to begin their search for the fated mate of Prince Adrian of the North."

Zale snorted, and Kai glanced over his shoulder at his brothers.

Marlin leaned toward Rian and elbowed him. "You're next, brother."

Rian raised his chin and sniffed. "I will do my duty as required."

"Of course you will," Caol murmured. "I'm so glad I'm the youngest."

"You are the youngest for now," Marlin said. "You never know. There's an unbonded omega still in the castle. Our father could very well take him for his very own and produce another heir. I think the ol' king still has a few knots left in him."

Kai groaned. Zale gagged. Caol released a muffled chuckle.

"Well, he's not *that* old yet," Marlin continued.

"Do you have something to share with the rest of us, son?" King Solomon bellowed across the Great Hall.

Marlin pinned his lips together before answering, "No." Then turned his face away to hide his laughter.

Kai turned toward the front of the hall to face the king. "Father, are we finished?"

"No. I have something else that needs said."

"Here we go, he's going to announce that he's taking that poor omega," Marlin whispered behind him.

The king continued, "I have judged your omega more harshly than I should have, Prince Kai. Your fated mate has not only survived the whelp of my first grandpup but has produced an alpha. Because of this, I have invited his parents, the alpha Nero and the omega Evian of Cascadia to join us in the Northern Colony."

"What?" whispered Luca.

Kai was just as shocked at that announcement as his mate.

He bounced Dylan in his arms and leaned closer to Luca. "Is that acceptable with you?"

Luca turned teary eyes toward Kai. "Yes! I would love that. I take back every bad thing I've ever said about your father."

"Don't be too hasty, my love. He's deserved everything you've sputtered in anger."

"I know, but... my parents! They'll get to live in the colony and help raise Dylan and get to watch him grow."

Kai smiled. "Our pup will be spoiled."

Luca wiped at his eyes and took a deep breath. "Of course he will!"

"Then I will have two sassy mouths in my household."

"Should I go give him a hug in thanks?"

"Who?" Kai asked, confused.

"The king!"

Zale leaned forward in between them. "Oh yes, please do. I want to see his face when you do that."

"No, you will not," Kai answered Luca, giving his brother a frown.

"I need to hug him," Luca insisted.

"No."

"Yes!" Zale encouraged.

"No, Omega, you will remain where you are," Kai commanded, trying to at least appear in control.

"No, my prince, I really need to hug him."

Suddenly, Luca took off toward the front of the Great Hall and Kai sighed loudly. Luca practically stumbled up the two steps to the throne.

Kai had to admit that look on the king's face was priceless when Luca caught his balance and then launched himself at King Solomon, wrapping his arms around Kai's father and squeezing him tightly.

The king's mouth hung agape as he appeared unsure of how to react or what to do.

Zale snickered behind Kai.

"Gotta love him," Caol said, laughing.

"I do. Very much," Kai finally said, then pinned his lips together to keep from bursting out in laughter.

IF YOU ENJOYED THIS BOOK

Thank you for reading The Selkie Prince's Fated Mate. If you enjoyed Kai and Luca's story, please consider leaving a review at your favorite retailer and/or Goodreads to let other readers know. Reviews are always appreciated and just a few words can help an independent author like me tremendously!

THE SELKIE PRINCE & HIS OMEGA GUARD

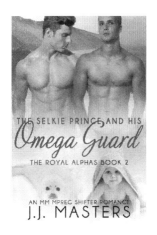

Turn the page to read the first chapter of book 2 of The Royal Alphas Series

Chapter One

PRINCE ADRIAN, the second born alpha son to the King of the North, frowned. As he stood near the throne where his father sat with his four brothers flanking him, his gaze bounced off the six omegas that had their foreheads pinned to the stone floor and their naked asses presented in the air.

He sighed quietly in disappointment. Not one of these omegas was his fated mate. The Selkie Seekers had gathered these males from good families all over the world, but none of the half dozen presented today belonged to him.

He glanced over at Luca who stood with his pup, Dylan, at the back of the Great Hall, bouncing the baby in his arms to keep him from fussing. Rian reminded himself that it had taken his oldest brother, Kai, several presentation ceremonies until he found his fated mate.

This was only his first. But still...

Unlike Kai, Rian had always preferred the Selkie traditions

and he looked forward to finding his true mate and producing an heir. He was tired of rutting with the betas they had at their disposal. And to even think about rutting with a human...

He wrinkled his nose. His brothers may very well enjoy the sexual release the human males brought, but Rian refused to join them. He was a Selkie prince. He would rut only with another Selkie.

He found humans to be boring and he figured none of them would be able to take his size anyway. As his brothers like to point out, time and time again, Rian was *big*. Most alphas were, but his was... extraordinary. As his younger brother Zale liked to call it... a dinosaur bone.

Not even all the betas could accommodate him. He knew which ones could and tended to use them for relief when needed.

He wrinkled his nose again, but this time it was for another reason. A sweet scent pulled at him. And it wasn't coming from any of the omegas kneeling on the ground before him.

His eyes flicked back to Luca. Then he twisted his head and glanced over his shoulder at Kai. "Is Luca due to come into oestrus soon?"

Kai's blue eyes narrowed as his gaze shot to his omega mate then back to Rian. "No."

Rian inhaled deeply trying to pinpoint what the smell was and where it was coming from. "Do you smell that?"

Before any of his brothers could answer him, this father, the king, loudly pounded the end of his scepter onto the floor at his feet.

"Douglass! If Prince Adrian cannot identify any of these omegas as his fated mate, then let's get this wrapped up."

His father's asshole assistant fluttered down the steps from where he had been standing behind the king, and approached Rian.

Rian frowned at the beta servant. "What?"

"Has none of them caught your fancy, Your Highness?"

Rian let his gaze wander over the six naked males all bent over in a line. "None of these are my omega, Douglass. You may dismiss them all." He tried to keep the disappointment out of his voice, but it was a struggle.

With a nod of his head and what curiously looked like a satisfied expression, Douglass clapped his hands, had the omegas rise to their feet, and herded them out of the Great Hall.

Rian couldn't help but take one last look at the naked men. All were from acceptable families, all very handsome and some were even hung very well for an omega, but even if he was sexually interested in any of them, he was forbidden to rut with them.

Doing so could throw an omega into heat and with heat came pregnancy and then Rian would be stuck with an omega who was not his intended fated mate.

All for a quick dalliance.

Rutting for pleasure with an omega would also ruin the omega's reputation. Omegas didn't have to come to their mate with their corona membrane intact, but no matter what, they couldn't rut with an alpha unless it was their mate. To do so was illegal and could mean imprisonment. Or worse, banishment.

For an omega, beta lovers were acceptable, alpha lovers were not. For an alpha, beta lovers were acceptable, omegas were not. The betas had the most freedom when it came to lovers, but they, unfortunately, were not fertile so could never produce pups, and would remain childless unless they adopted one, which was rare since they were only permitted to adopt orphaned beta pups.

As he turned to address his father, the somewhat strangely familiar scent hit him again. It wasn't strong, but it was enough to make his cock twitch in his pants.

Rian quickly glanced around. No omega now remained in the Great Hall besides Luca and if Luca wasn't in heat, then...

"Are we done here, father?" Caol, Rian's youngest brother, asked impatiently. "I have things I need to do."

"You mean males you need to do," Zale corrected.

"No, I actually have some royal duties to attend to," Caol answered.

"Royal duties?" Marlin scoffed, then he practically fell off the platform that held the throne when he doubled over laughter.

"Whatever, brother. Father, are we done?" Caol asked again.

With a sigh, King Solomon raised his hand and waved it. "Go. All of you, just go."

Caol jogged down the steps and rushed out of the hall.

"Someone must have a hot date," Kai murmured as he wandered down the steps at a slower pace. He paused next to Rian and clapped his hand on Rian's shoulder. "Sorry, brother, I know you hoped to only have to do this once. Your mate's out there, I'm sure of it."

Rian nodded as his older brother headed toward his own bonded mate and pup.

Suddenly, Douglass was back, flitting around the king, assisting him from the throne and helping him with the heavy scepter. He even reached up and adjusted the king's crown when it tilted precariously on his head. "Your Royal Highness, let me assist you back to your quarters."

"He's not an invalid, Dougie," Marlin said. "He's quite spry for his age."

The king shot his second youngest son a look. "You make me sound ancient."

"Father, I know you're not. And I know you've been keeping that omega in the wings just for yourself."

King Solomon's dark blue eyes narrowed as he stepped up to his son and pulled himself to his full height. "You forget yourself, *Prince Marlin*."

Marlin dipped his head then met his father's gaze head-on.

"So tell us that you don't intend to take Finn as your own mate. You know it's dangerous to keep him in the castle when he's not bonded to an alpha. My suggestion is to send him back to his colony and his family."

"Good thing I don't rule this colony with your suggestions."

Marlin "hmm'd," then said, "Well, it's a good suggestion," before heading toward the exit. "At least let Dr. Harper put him on heat suppressants so we all don't fight over him when he comes into heat."

"I'll consider it," the king answered dryly.

Rian surprisingly agreed with his brother. He had no idea why the king hadn't sent the unbonded omega away. He had only brought Finn to the colony when he wasn't sure that Luca could get pregnant. He'd been on the verge of making Kai's mate an outcast and forcing his oldest brother to take that omega instead.

His father was all about making sure their royal bloodline continued and that there would always be an heir to sit on the throne when his stubborn ass finally gave it up.

Which wouldn't be any time soon.

With five alpha sons, even Rian, who also didn't want to see their bloodline die out, agreed that the king in no way needed another omega or to bear a sixth son. He already lost five omegas during whelp. Kai even had nicknamed him the Black Widow of the Selkies. Because of his father's unlucky streak when it came to mates, none of his brothers had the same *pater*.

As Rian watched his father and Marlin leave the Great Hall, he wondered why he wasn't moving to leave as well.

For some reason he couldn't. The alluring scent that wafted around him kept him frozen in place. It didn't make any sense.

Luca wasn't in heat. Finn wasn't either. Even if he was, the visiting omega hardly left his quarters, which was as far from the prince's wings as it could be.

The only males remaining in the Great Hall were the Royal Guards.

He let his gaze roam over the dozen betas that lined both sides of the hall. None, of course, made eye contact. They stood staring straight ahead, stiff as a board, all holding spears.

Yes, *spears*. Because his father refused to allow the guards to carry guns. Which was a bit ridiculous for this modern day and age. Though they at least carried a large knife on their belt and were trained in hand-to-hand combat, that was it.

If he was king...

Rian sighed. He would never be king. And neither would his firstborn son.

But that still didn't mean he didn't want to do his duty and produce an heir. *Just in case.*

Not that he wished ill will on Kai or his son, Dylan, he didn't.

The sweet scent tickled his nose again, making his cock twitch once more and start to grow this time.

That made no sense. Betas made up the Royal Guard for a reason. And that reason was a sound one. They wouldn't react to any omega in oestrus, nor did they come into heat themselves. And the only alphas permitted as their leaders had to already be bonded to an omega mate. And even then, there were only a handful of those.

The alpha guard standing at the front of the hall bowed deeply at the waist as Rian approached him. "Your Royal Highness, can I dismiss the guards?"

"Not yet."

The alpha tipped his dark head and returned to standing at attention. Rian turned on his heels at the front of the hall and stared down the line of guards.

Something was amiss, and he didn't like it.

How had his brothers not smelled that odor? That sweet, intoxicating aroma that remained in the hall.

Rian cross his arms behind his back and marched down the line of guards to the right of the throne, taking his time, pausing for a split moment in front of each one, giving them a good once over, then moving on to the next in line. When he was done with the six on the one side of the hall he crossed over to the other side and started at the end doing the same. Pause, sniff, a thorough once over.

Then it hit him like a stone wall. The second one in. His step stuttered as he pulled himself to a halt. He planted his feet so he wouldn't lean in and shove his face against the guard's neck to take a deeper inhale.

He gritted his teeth since his erection was now raging and he clenched his hands into fists to keep himself under control.

This beta had an odd scent. An enticing odor. One he never smelled before on a beta.

It wasn't quite like when Luca had gone into heat. That aroma had been almost impossible to resist and if Luca hadn't already bonded with Kai, not only Rian but all his brothers would have fought to the death to rut and breed with Luca. The scent given off during oestrus had a purpose, which was to ensure the continuation of their species.

However, the scent of one's intended fated mate when not in oestrus was still detectable but not nearly as strong. But the scent would be just potent enough for an alpha to identify his fated mate. The omega who was destined to bear that alpha's pups.

Or in his case, the possible heirs to the throne.

Since most fated mates were strangers and must rut during the bonding ceremony, that identifying pheromones made them extremely appealing to each other, making the entire process much easier on both Selkies. An attraction they both couldn't resist.

His attention was drawn back to the guard in question. Rian turned to face him directly and inspected him from head to toe.

He was tall. Taller than most betas and even some alphas. He was very handsome with light brown hair and chocolate brown eyes. And it was clear to Rian the guard was trying not to meet his gaze.

Rian's nostrils flared as he inhaled deeply once again.

That was a colossal mistake. When that unique aroma entered his lungs, he shuddered and fought the urge to touch himself as well.

His reaction was frightening. While some betas could turn him on, and he'd rutted with enough of them, he'd never reacted to one like this before. Usually to get this hard with a beta, he needed to work at it.

Maybe he should have this guard removed from his current duties and moved into the king's stable for his use. Of course, the male would need to agree to it. None of the betas at their sexual disposal were forced. They were all volunteers and got to live a pampered life in exchange.

He pursed his lips. Would this one be agreeable?

He would love to explore this desire further. In private.

Rian closed his eyes and blew out a breath. What the hell was he thinking? He was turning into Caol, whose goal was to rut with every beta and human male on the planet. Or at least in the northeast.

He was a prince, not a rutting fool. There was no good reason to remove a guard from his duties just for his pleasure.

None whatsoever.

But the male's lips... They looked full and soft and so... kissable, among other things.

Rian straightened, appalled at where his thoughts were headed. He stiffly turned and rushed down the line of the remaining guards and went directly to their alpha leader.

He tried to keep his voice level as he commanded, "You may now dismiss the guards, but you must remain."

The alpha guard bowed his head once again. "Yes, Your Royal Highness." He lifted his head and shouted, "Fall out."

As one, the guards turned on their heels and filed out of the Great Hall in an orderly fashion as they were trained to do. As soon as Rian heard the double doors at the end of the hall latch, he inquired, "The last guard I stopped at, he's a beta?"

"Yes, Your Royal Highness. As you well know, the captain only employs betas as guards. That is law."

"You haven't detected anything strange about him?"

"Your Highness, has he offended you in some way? If so, I—"

"No!" Rian cut him off. He did not want to see a beta lose his job because of his own wild imagination. "No," he continued more calmly. "But instruct the captain to remove that guard from duty in the Great Hall. From the castle all together. If he has any questions regarding that order, please have him come see me."

"Again, Your Highness, if he's insulted in you in some way..."

"He has not. He may remain in our service, but just have him moved elsewhere. That is all." Rian waved his hand. "Carry on with the rest of your day. I thank you for your service."

The alpha guard tapped his heels together. "Thank you, Your Highness."

Rian waited until the male left the cavernous room. He finally let his hand wander to his painful erection and he stroked it over his pants.

"Holy Poseidon," he muttered as his hips twitched in an automatic response to his own touch. He needed to relieve his erection and the deep ache in his balls.

With an annoyed sigh, he headed toward the quarters where the betas lived within the compound.

He only hoped that one of the betas who could accommodate his size was available and willing.

If not, he would have to tackle his enormous problem on his own.

Learn more about book 2 in The Royal Alphas series here: http://www.jjmastersauthor.com/p/the-selkie-princes-alpha-royals-series.html

ABOUT THE AUTHOR

J.J. Masters is the alter-ego of a USA Today bestselling author who love to write hot, gay romance. J.J. became fascinated with Mpreg romance as soon as she figured out what mpreg stood for.

You can join JJ's FB Group or her newsletter to keep up with exclusive content and news.

Author Links:
Website: http://www.jjmasterauthor.com
FB Fan Group:
https://www.facebook.com/groups/JJMastersAuthor/
Newsletter: https://bit.ly/2E2zcaB

f facebook.com/JJMastersAuthor

twitter.com/JJMastersAuthor

instagram.com/jjmastersauthor

Made in the USA
Columbia, SC
30 September 2019